Violet for Bonaparte

Geoffrey Trease is well known as a writer in several fields,
having adult novels and non-fiction books to his credit as
well as many stories for young people.

Mr Trease has had a lifelong passion for history, and has
written many historical novels for the young. He has also
travelled widely, mainly in Europe, but his writing comes first
and he spends much of his time at his desk. He lives with his
wife in a delightful house on the slopes of the Malvern Hills.

Geoffrey Trease

Violet for Bonaparte

cover illustration by Chris Molan

Piccolo Pan Books
in association with Macmillan London

First published 1976 by Macmillan London Ltd
This edition published 1978 by Pan Books Ltd,
Cavaye Place, London SW10 9PG
in association with Macmillan London Ltd
© Geoffrey Trease 1976
ISBN 0 330 25490 1
Printed in Great Britain by
Cox & Wyman Ltd, London, Reading and Fakenham

Contents

1 News from Paris

'Hang you?' echoed Linfoot in that bluff way he had. He puffed out his mauve cheeks. The hooded eyes narrowed further to wicked twinkling slits. ' 'Course they'll hang you! Or I'll know the reason why. Month from now – all London will be gaping at you.'

Ben shivered.

It was still only early April, and the winter of 1814 had been the hardest in memory. There had been a cheerful coal fire; now it had sunk low, forgotten. The day outside was bright, but Linfoot used this room because no morning sunshine entered it.

Ben had cause to shiver. He was wearing only an antique Grecian helmet, winged sandals, and a scrap of cloth around his middle. Yet move an inch, and an angry squawk from the old man would petrify him to absolute stillness again.

'You're as good as finished,' said Linfoot jovially. 'One more session. Have to have you framed, then. And varnished. Just before the exhibition opens.' He studied the canvas with critical approval. 'Rest,' he said. 'And make up the fire.'

Thankfully Ben stepped off the dais, laid down sword and helmet, and padded across. There was still a welcome glow to greet his chest and thighs as he crouched, building up fresh coals. He rose, huddling into the threadbare dressing-gown Linfoot kept for his models. The old man turned from the cupboard, decanter in hand.

'Glass of madeira, me boy? Warm us up.'

'Oh – thank you, sir.'

Surprised, Ben took the glass. Linfoot was not often so considerate. When inspired, he worked like a demon, despite his age. It was not that he was unaware of his models as human beings. He would talk to them volubly – about art, about the foreign countries he had visited in his youth, about the stupidities of the government, the wickedness of Bonaparte, and the impossible behaviour of the Americans. To all this the models must listen and make intelligent response, moving only the lips. They were paid a shilling an hour, weren't they? Surely they could stand still for that.

Ben was not one to grumble. He loved the old man's talk. Often he did not agree with his dogmatic opinions – about the proper subjects for painters, say, or those impossible Americans, for whom Ben felt a sneaking sympathy – but he knew better than to answer back. He let Linfoot's words flow over him. Linfoot had lived so long, seen so much. Italy, France before the Revolution, the awful Alps . . .

Linfoot was back at his easel, gloating.

'This'll show 'em!'

'Yes, sir.'

'They think I'm past it.' Linfoot bent, creakily, peering at the lower part of the picture, where the waves curled round the rock. He chuckled like an angry parrot. 'Been in the Academy too long. Not in the mode. Bah! Good painting is good painting. And you're the right model for Perseus,' he added generously. 'Lucky day when I took that stroll at Chelsea.'

Lucky for me, too, thought Ben. Lucky that I fancied a swim and he saw me as I came up the bank.

Soon it would be two years. Since then, he had posed for several big classical pictures, not to mention countless pencil sketches. The money was good and the hours convenient: Linfoot worked in the mornings and stage-hands weren't needed at the theatre until the evening.

And there was Linfoot's talk, better than any schooling. Ben had never had much schooling, and he hungered for it. Linfoot had been intrigued from their first meeting.

'Tell me, lad,' he had demanded, 'I know where you get your muscles – heaving scenery about at Covent Garden – but where do you get your *words*? Your father's doorman at the theatre, you live in this alley off the Strand, yet you have almost the diction of a gentleman.'

Ben had felt shy but pleased. 'I suppose, sir, it comes from the theatre – like the muscles.'

8

'Ah! You listen.'

Certainly Ben listened. Standing in the wings, night after night, he banqueted on language. Shakespeare, Sheridan, Goldsmith, a host of authors . . . Splendid words, spoken by splendid people: Kemble, Sarah Siddons until her recent retirement, a dazzling list of famous players . . .

He could never understand the other scene-shifters. They lounged in the shadows, whispering about race-horses and prize-fighters, impatient for the final curtain and the first tankard of ale round the corner. All that poetry and wit passed them by.

Now Linfoot's brisk voice recalled him to the present. 'Ready?'

'Yes, sir.' Ben put down the empty glass, dropped the dressing-gown and resumed the pose, putting on the appropriate expression – half horror, half admiration – of Perseus discovering Andromeda. Thanks to Linfoot, he now knew the legend well.

The left half of the canvas was occupied by the maiden, cowering against the rock to which she was chained to await the dragon, her long hair streaming down to veil her nakedness.

He could not help wondering about Andromeda – the model, not the heroine of antiquity. He did not know her real name. Linfoot did not like his models to meet, even to pass on the stairs. 'The young woman attends on Wednesdays and Fridays,' he had explained dryly, 'so on those days you will not be required.'

Next month, when the fashionable crowds flocked to Somerset House for the Academy exhibition, they would be seeing, as they admired Linfoot's *Perseus and Andromeda*, a young man and a girl who had never set eyes on each other and probably never would.

Perhaps as well, Ben consoled himself. It could have been embarrassing.

He had long given up speculating why Perseus should have set forth on his adventures in nothing but his magical helmet and sandals. He knew now that it was the regulation dress of this particular hero.

'See it from the artist's point of view,' Linfoot would explain enthusiastically. 'Flesh is alive. Nerves, muscles, infinite variation! Armour's all right – it glints, yes, you can do interesting things with light and shade—'

'Chiaroscuro?' Ben had suggested, proud of the Italian word.

'That's it, lad!' Linfoot had been pleased. 'Drapery, too – I like drapery sometimes. Sweep, flow, texture, transparency! But nothing equals the human form as God designed it.'

So, patient, obedient, but already getting chilly again, Ben kept his stance on the low dais, staring into nothingness as though the unclad Andromeda were shrinking with downcast eyes not two yards away.

'Fine,' Linfoot was muttering. 'Ten more minutes. Then we'll break for today. Finish you next time.' He fiddled with his palette. 'Perhaps a little more brightness in the eye? Yes.' He dabbed, stood back, squinted at picture and model alternately, stepped forward and with infinite delicacy dabbed again. 'Got it! As the poet tells us—'

He began to recite, as he loved to do, rolling out the Latin verses drummed into him at Harrow half a century before. Ben understood not a word, but he enjoyed the beat of the hexameters.

Neither of them heard the patter of feet on the stairs, and when the door burst open they were taken completely by surprise.

Linfoot spun round, arms spread, scandalized.

'Emma! How *dare* you? How often have I told you, child?'

The girl stood in the doorway, breathless, radiating excitement.

'I'm sorry, Grandpapa! But the *news*! I had to tell you the news.'

2 Sandals with wings

'News?' Linfoot almost exploded. 'What news? You burst in without knocking – when I am painting from the life—'

He glanced back to the dais. But Ben had dived for the screen behind which he had left his clothes. From there, hopping frantically as he strove to dress, hampered by the sandals he had forgotten at first to remove, he heard Emma Linfoot proclaim: 'Napoleon has given in!'

'He *has*?'

Her grandfather began to caper rapturously, brush in hand, a quaint figure from a bygone period, for the old artist ignored change. He retained the silk stockings and the knee-breeches of the last century, detesting these new-fangled trousers – no dress for a gentleman – and vowing he would keep his powdered wig if he were the last in England to do so.

'Yes, Grandpapa. It's taken from the Paris newspapers. He's given up his throne, he's going into exile—'

'Ought to be shot!' snorted Linfoot. 'All these years – battle after battle – sacrificing thousands of innocent lives—'

'But it's over now! I'm sorry I broke in upon you, but—'

'You are forgiven, Emma.' Linfoot cackled at a sudden thought. 'After all, you've seen nothing – have you?'

An awkward silence hung briefly in the room while Miss Linfoot struggled breathlessly to frame a truthful but satisfactory answer. At length her grandfather took pity on her.

'Have you forgotten all I taught you about the Greek legends?' he demanded with mock severity. 'Perseus and Andromeda: what was the magic property of his helmet?'

'Oh – er – *I* know! It rendered him invisible!' Emma began to giggle. 'I see.'

'You do not see,' he corrected her, 'nor *have* you seen – anything or anybody – save an elderly artist, desperately striving to finish his picture for the Academy next month.'

'No, Grandpapa.' She was trying hard to control her laughter.

'Run along now. I'll be down directly. We must celebrate. God knows, we have waited long enough.'

'Yes, Grandpapa.' Ben, decent now in shirt and breeches, peeped round the screen. The girl lingered, her hand on the doorknob. 'You realize what this means?' she said.

'I should, me dear. Peace in Europe.'

'And Jane's father free!' She was transfigured with joy.

'And not the only one! Yes, we may thank God indeed.' He clapped his hands impatiently. 'Off with you, child!' And the white door swung softly shut behind her.

It was obviously the end of work for that day. Linfoot pottered about the room, cleaning his brushes. As Ben emerged from shelter, he remarked with a chuckle, 'You must excuse my impulsive granddaughter. It's a great day for all of us.'

'It is indeed, sir!'

'Miss Emma has special cause for rejoicing. She has an old school-friend – very close. Poor Miss Faraday's father was touring on the Continent years ago – that short break after the treaty at Amiens, when everyone rushed headlong abroad – but I suppose you won't remember?'

'I was quite a little chap, sir.'

'Bless me soul, you must have been. Yes. 1802.'

'Twelve years ago.'

'Twelve? Gracious! Well, the very next year, this wretched Bonaparte began meddling in Italy. The war flared up suddenly. Hundreds of our tourists were caught. He interned them as prisoners – even harmless civilians like Mr Faraday. They've been kept at Verdun ever since.'

'No wonder Miss Linfoot is delighted for her friend.'

'Yes . . .' But Linfoot's mind had raced on. 'Europe open once more! People will travel again – after all this time. See Rome, Venice, Florence . . . Wonderful!'

'Will *you*, sir?'

Linfoot shook his head. 'No, me boy, it's come too late. I remember those appalling roads. Dreadful inns, heat and flies – and worst of all, the foreigners! Touring is for younger men.' He pondered. 'I was in Paris when the Revolution started. Twenty-five years ago. Twenty-five years!' He counted four shillings into Ben's palm. 'Four hours,' he said in a brisker tone. 'Wednesday morning, then. With luck, we should finish.'

Going downstairs, Ben heard excited chatter from the drawing-room. For once he was relieved not to run into Miss Linfoot, though normally he would have enjoyed the encounter. Emma was a girl to brighten anyone's day. He never mentioned her to Sal. Sal might have misunderstood.

As he walked homewards to the Strand, he could sense the mounting fever of the city. Strangers were greeting each other. Crowds clustered round anyone with a newspaper. Servants were out on balconies or poised on ladders, putting out flags and garlands and draperies. Huge coloured transparencies were being stretched across the frontages, ready to be lit from behind when darkness fell. Even private houses were hanging smaller versions in their windows.

The theatre was not likely to be outdone. When he got home to Somerset Alley, Ben was not surprised to be greeted by a flustered mother.

'Here you are, lad! Best get your dinner down you, double quick. Your dad's just sent word from the theatre. They need the lot of you.'

'I'll lay they do.' Ben dropped easily into a different language when he returned to Somerset Alley. He attacked the stew she set before him, wiped his lips as the last mouthful disappeared, crammed on his hat again, and fled.

A smiling Sal barred his passage as he reached the Strand.

That was the trouble with Sal. You never knew when you might run into her. She worked at a milliner's in Fleet Street, and, as one of the junior girls, was often sent out on errands.

Sal was all right. A good sort. Undeniably pretty. Other lads envied him. But of late she'd taken to behaving as though Ben belonged to her. He didn't. And he wasn't sure he ever meant to.

'Benjie!'

'Sal! Can't stop – I'm wanted at the theatre—'

'*This* time o' day?'

'It's to fix the decorations outside – for the victory—'

'Isn't it wonderful, Benjie? The town will be a sight when they're all lit up. I wondered—'

'Yes?'

'When you finish tonight – would you take me round to see everything?'

'If you like – 'course I will.'

'I do like. Thank you, Benjie.'

He detached himself and dived across the road, under the very noses of the horses. He would be glad to take Sal to see the illuminations. She was always at her best where there was some excitement. It was easier when they had something definite to do. Sustained conversation never went so well, for she did not share his interests. There was only one topic she was inclined to discuss seriously, but when he caught the first hint of *that*, he did his best to head her off.

At the theatre he found a scene of pandemonium unusual at that early hour. The stage-manager pounced upon him.

'Ah! Young Reeth! You fancy yourself as an artist!'

Ben's artistic interests were a good-natured joke among the men back-stage. Not only was it well known that he modelled for a famous Royal Academician, but his own amateur sketches were sometimes handed round, frankly criticized and occasionally admired. When the regular scene-painters needed help with the rough work, it was Ben they called upon.

He went over.

Two painters were busy on a vast stretch of linen. He saw at once that it was no ordinary drop-scene but a transparency. They were using not their usual opaque paints but the translucent dyes that became visible only when the cloth was brightly illuminated from behind. He had more than once taken a hand in such a job, invaluable when a play or pantomime called for trickwork, such as sunsets and fires and volcanic eruptions.

This time, however, the transparency was wanted for display outside the theatre, and that very evening.

One painter was frenziedly daubing in a gigantic figure of

Britannia. His colleague was equally absorbed in the depiction of a cringing Napoleon.

This man paused only to growl, 'We need Elba. In the background. You can manage that.'

'Elba?'

'This place they're sending him to.'

'But what's it *like*?'

'How the devil should I know? And what does it matter? It's an island. Off Italy. Small. Use your imagination. If I finish Boney in time, I'll print *Elba* over it – don't *you* try lettering! Any sort of blotch will do for an island.'

Ben set to work. He was not going to be satisfied with a blotch. Though he had never heard of the island before today, he would produce something worthy of this great occasion. The result was strongly reminiscent of *Robinson Crusoe*. No one had time to argue. The April twilight was gathering outside, and the other stage-hands were waiting to hang the great cloth in position.

Sal, if no one else, professed greatly to admire his handiwork when late that evening, the performance over, she stood clutching his arm amid the gaping crowd in Bow Street.

'You are *clever*, Benjie!'

'Good Lord, that's nothing.'

He had done his best, and he liked praise, as well as the next, but not when it was uncritical and based on ignorance. It had been a rush job. Anyhow, this sort of painting gave you no chance to be subtle. He thought of the folio of sketches he had taken to show Linfoot last week. Had the old man found time to look at the efforts of an untaught amateur?

'Well, they must think highly of you at the theatre,' Sal insisted, as they pushed their way through Covent Garden. 'They ought to put your money up.'

'I don't know, Sal—'

'Many a young lad like you would be thinking of getting wed. It's only natural. He'd be needing enough for a wife, and then a family.'

'Some might,' he admitted uneasily.

They had reached the Strand. The street was packed with a

slowly moving multitude, singing, cheering, sometimes even booing, as when they stared up at a huge transparency displayed outside Akerman's, entitled *The Corsican Attacked by Death.*

The illuminations were certainly worth seeing. There were victorious Britannias and discomfited Napoleons on every side. There were gallant allies, old Blücher and his Prussian king and the Emperor of Russia, portrayed in a four-horse chariot. Even the rightful King of France, fat and gouty Louis XVIII, who had been living snug in Buckinghamshire, doing less than any one to defeat the usurper and regain his crown, was politely remembered. And of course there were Britain's own heroes: the Iron Duke's portrait encircled by laurels, and those like Nelson and Pitt who, alas, had not lived to see this day.

Ben wished that Sal would be content to enjoy the display, but when Sal had an idea in her mind, she was like a dog with a bone.

' 'Course,' she said, coming back to the subject, 'even now I s'pose you *could* get wed – if – if you fancied anyone. With what Mr Linfoot pays you, and he's not the only painter, and your steady job at the theatre—'

'I don't know as I'll stay at the theatre.'

'Not *stay*?' she exclaimed. Even through his thick sleeve he felt the alarm in the sudden clutch of her little fingers. Like a bird's talons they were.

He glanced down at her face, pretty in its frame of ringlets, but pallid in the lamplight, and threatening thunder.

'I . . . I don't know,' he said clumsily. He edged forward through the crowd. She had to move with him, like a boat in tow.

How could he explain to her? He did not want to be tied down to the theatre. Or, come to that, to be tied down to anything – or anybody. Yet.

Listening to old Linfoot had opened his mind to new ideas. Especially during this past month or two. It was as though in binding on the magic sandals of Perseus he had acquired some of that hero's adventurous instincts. He might have no wings, but even mortal feet could carry one about the world. Until this morning, his yearnings had been vague and hopeless. Then had come the news from France, and the old artist's cry, 'Europe open once more!' Followed by the wistful afterthought, 'Touring is for younger men.'

'Come on,' he said, drawing her along towards Fleet Street, 'they say the best of all is at Ludgate Hill. Blades, the glassmakers – they've put up something special—'

'Never mind Blades! I want to know what's in your mind. Leaving the theatre!'

'I've not decided. But – I'd like to move around and see a few places. Before I settle down. With the war over, it'll be possible to travel again.'

'Travel? What do *you* want to travel for?'

'Oh . . . all sorts of things. I'd like to see some of the places old Linfoot talks about. Venice – and the picture-galleries – and the monuments of antiquity—'

'Old Linfoot's a monument of antiquity himself!' she said viciously.

'He's a very decent old gentleman. He's taught me a lot.'

'He's filled your head with a lot of nonsense! You're an ordinary young workman, Benjie, not one of these artists.'

'Mr Turner was only the son of the barber in Maiden Lane, a stone's throw from us. Look at him now!'

But Sal knew little and cared less about that illustrious member of the Royal Academy.

'Anyway you've not got the money to go travelling,' she said with obvious relief. 'That's only for the gentry.'

'Gentry need servants.' Her opposition stung him to find answers. What had been a formless notion began to take shape. 'I'd try anything, if it gave me the chance to see Italy.'

'Servants are trained. What use would *you* be?' she jeered. 'A footman? A valet? There's good experienced men needing a place. Lining up, hat in hand, they are, with references from the best families.'

'Maybe you're right.' He did not want to argue, and spoil what had been meant as a little pleasure-jaunt. 'It was just an idea.' He grinned. 'And now I've a better one.'

'What?' She was not to be won over at once.

'Let's get out of this crush. Find a tavern, and drink to the victory.'

'That'd be nice. Somewhere respectable, mind.'

He knew just the place. Fit to take any self-respecting young woman, though on this night of nights it might be noisier than usual. That might be a good thing. The one danger of sitting down in a quiet place with Sal was that she'd bring conversation round to the same old dangerous subject.

They had first to pass the offices of the Gaslight Company, and here the throng stood thicker than anywhere they had been.

The reason was obvious. Keen to advertise its wonderful modern invention, the company had mounted a display that was drawing gasps of admiration from all sides. On the front of the building an artificial tree had been set up. It had leaves like laurel and a profusion of brilliant blossoms which quivered like jets of golden flame.

'Look! They *are* flame,' he told Sal.

'Oooh! Isn't it wonderful?'

In the glow of those fiery blossoms mere lamps and candles looked dim. The novelty held the crowd spellbound. Some had never seen gaslighting before.

Ben and Sal were brought to a standstill. Directly in front of them, solid as the Rock of Gibraltar and perhaps (thought Ben) not much smaller, was a burly gentleman who would have made a perfect model for John Bull. He was staring up at the tree of fire, rapt in contemplation, his broad shoulders and tall top hat completely blocking Sal's view.

Ben edged gently to the left, trying to make a space from which the girl could see without obstruction. It was just as he did so, lowering his eyes when everyone else was gaping upwards, that he saw the pickpocket.

It was neat, instantaneous, as good as any conjuring trick he had seen on a stage.

A barefoot boy bumped into the stout gentleman, who cursed him loudly. As he turned his head to do so, a ragged fellow appeared suddenly on his other side. Ben had a momentary glimpse of the pocket-book as its glossy leather caught the radiant gaslight. Then it vanished into the out-stretched paw of a third figure in shirt-sleeves and a striped waistcoat.

The stout gentleman roared and spun round in time to clutch the ragged fellow. Ben did not wait to see what happened. He let go Sal's arm and clove his way through the crowd behind him, in determined pursuit of the striped waistcoat.

3 Sir Henry

The fugitive was small and slipped through the press of sight-seers with the deftness of experience. Ben was big, but he was also determined. His height allowed him to keep the tousled head in view and his weight forced a clear passage through the protesting crowd.

At first the thief did not know he was being followed. He was moving fast, but not too fast, so as not to arouse suspicion. Ben, on the other hand, had no reason for concealment. With muttered apologies, but without slackening his pace, he forged ahead, and brought his hands down on the striped waistcoat just as its wearer dived into a side-turning.

'Here!' the thief squealed indignantly.

'No, *here*,' Ben corrected him firmly. He took the wallet into his own left hand, holding the captive painfully by the scruff of the neck with the other.

The nearest bystanders turned their attention from the gas-light display to the counter-attraction of a frustrated pick-pocket. At the same moment the hubbub along the street rose to such a pitch that a murder seemed imminent. Furious voices were raised. Heads were bobbing, hats flying. There were feminine screams. A swooning lady was being carried, with difficulty, to safety.

'By your leave, gentlemen,' said Ben. 'The owner is just over there.' He slipped the wallet into his own breeches-pocket, for his wriggling prisoner required both his hands, and began to push his way back.

Sal hailed him thankfully, her big eyes looking bigger with alarm. '*Quick*, Benjie! Or they'll do something dreadful!'

The ragged man who had actually taken the wallet was struggling in the grip of its owner, fervently protesting his innocence and calling upon the crowd to save him. Several bystanders laid restraining hands upon the angry gentleman. He shook them off contemptuously and bellowed that he would tear his captive limb from limb.

'I ain't got nothink o' his! Search me!'

One quick-witted spectator took up the suggestion. He ran deft fingers over the scarecrow figure.

'He's telling the truth,' he announced. 'He's got no wallet.' Looking sternly at the stout gentleman, he said, 'I'm afraid you've picked on the wrong man, sir. And you really ought not to be treating him in this violent fashion.'

There was a murmur of agreement. Sympathy swung to the terrified captive. 'You could have the law on him,' advised a clerk from the Temple close by.

'That's it,' cried another. 'Wrongful arrest!'

More voices chimed in with various suggestions.

'Assault and battery!'

'Breach of the peace!'

'Defamation of character!'

The stout gentleman was not impressed. 'Go to the devil, all of you!' he thundered. 'I *know* he took it.'

Loud though his voice was, it was drowned in the roar of opposition. A minute ago, most had been ready to fall upon the suspect. Now they surged round the accuser. Sheer weight of numbers might have overwhelmed him if Ben had not reached his side in time. As it was, the ragged man seized his chance and was gone.

'Hold on, gentlemen – *if* you please!' Ben shouted desperately. 'That fellow did take the wallet – I saw him. But he slipped it to his mate here.'

He shoved the striped-waistcoated accomplice in front of him and brandished the wallet for all to see. It meant letting go with one hand, and the thief was not going to miss a chance like that. Ben felt an excruciating hack on the shin, yelped and staggered off balance. He found himself dangling an empty waistcoat.

Fortunately his other hand still held the wallet, and this evidence convinced the crowd. Sympathy swung back to the stout gentleman and the tall young stranger who had recovered his property. No one questioned Ben's account of what he had seen. There was only regret that the villains had escaped.

'And who the devil's to blame for that?' demanded the stout gentleman.

At this point the bystanders began to drift away, remembering the lateness of the hour and the many illuminations they had yet to see. Ben and Sal found themselves alone with the wallet-owner. His massive face was still flushed, but it seemed his natural colour. He became genial.

'Vastly obliged to you, young man, vastly obliged.' He delved into his pocket, then hesitated with obvious embarrassment. 'Can't thank you properly here and now. Mustn't detain you. Can see you've other fish to fry.' He looked admiringly at Sal, who smiled back, far prettier than any fish that was ever fried. 'Just tell me where you live. Like to express my appreciation – some fitting manner—'

'There's no need, sir. Any honest person—'

'Perhaps. No matter, I insist.' His tone indicated that he was not accustomed to contradiction. 'Tell you what. Come and see me at Garland's Hotel. Tomorrow. After breakfast. Ask for Sir Henry Hawthorn.'

'If you wish, sir.'

'Won't keep you now, then.' Sir Henry beamed down at Sal. It was almost a leer. 'Run along. Enjoy yourselves. Be good.' His chuckle was a plain encouragement to the opposite. He turned away, and they watched his top hat and broad shoulders moving through the throng of smaller men.

'*Sir* Henry.' Sal was impressed. 'He might be ever so

useful, Benjie. Mind you go and see him tomorrow.'

'I've promised. I couldn't very well refuse.'

'I should think not! It was smart of you, not letting on where you live.'

'Smart? I didn't want him sending me a reward.'

'You *are* simple, Benjie,' she said impatiently. 'Anyhow, the hotel's best. I mean, Somerset Alley isn't much of an address.'

'It's good enough for my parents,' he told her curtly. 'And good enough for me.'

Having no session with Linfoot next morning, he was quite free to pay his call upon Sir Henry. Garland's was in the Haymarket, a favourite hotel (he knew) with the country gentry, just as ships' captains frequented the Tavistock in Covent Garden and Guards officers went to Stephen's in Bond Street.

Sir Henry was in the coffee-room, having just worked his way through a breakfast worthy of his size and not likely to reduce it. Having disposed of fried eggs and sausages, cold ham and beef, a plateful of bread and butter, and a capacious pot of mahogany-coloured tea, he rose reluctantly from the table, flung his napkin to the floor, and came out, clutching his newspaper. He was, Ben guessed, in his mid-forties. Even taller than Ben himself and vastly broader. His face broke into a smile of recognition. Thrusting out an arm like an oak-branch, he steered Ben into an empty room opposite.

'Ha! Our spry young fellow from last night – what's-ye-name—'

'Reeth, Sir Henry. Benjamin Reeth.'

'H'm. Now I can see you properly. Didn't know quite what to make of you then.' Sir Henry stood, feet squarely planted apart, summing up his visitor through small pale eyes.

Ben knew what was in his mind.

Last night, in the deceptive lights of Fleet Street, Sir Henry had been puzzled by the way he spoke. He had been doubtful of Ben's class, and, for fear of offending him, had left his guineas jingling in his pocket. Now, in the clear light of morning, he could see Ben for what he was, just a simply but decently dressed young workman.

'Well, Reeth,' he said. 'I'd like to show my appreciation in some way—'

'I don't want anything, thank you, sir.'

'The sentiment does you credit! But I insist. It wasn't just my wallet. Those fools would have had me down – they'd have taken that scallywag's word against mine, confound them—'

'There was a general misunderstanding – it was all extremely regrettable – very distasteful to a gentleman—'

'Regrettable? Distasteful? You may say so. And, dammit, you *do*. The way you express yourself, your words, your manner – you have me properly foxed, my boy. Have you come down in the world? Explain yourself. What do you do?'

With a smile, Ben told him about his work and his home. Far from coming down in the world, the Reeths felt they had risen a little. His father had come to London as a labourer. Now, as doorman at the grand new theatre in Covent Garden, he held a position of some responsibility.

'And what about *you*, eh? You mean to go beyond scene-shifting and modelling for painters?'

'That's in the lap of the gods, sir.'

'Is it? Is it, now?' Sir Henry glared at him, but somehow it was a friendly glare. 'I've taken a fancy to you, my boy. You're a handy fellow. I could use you. God knows just how. I shall think of something. Trouble is . . .'

'Sir?'

'Now the Continent is open at last, I've a mind to go abroad and travel.' He gave an anxious, sidelong look. 'That wouldn't do for you, I suppose?'

It was Ben's turn to hesitate. Curiosity and temptation were at war with caution. If Sir Henry had found him hard to sum up, he too did not know quite what to make of Sir Henry.

'Er – what had you in mind, sir?'

'Oh, France – Italy – the usual round people made before all this Napoleon nonsense.'

'I mean, sir – are you offering me some sort of employment?'

' 'Course I am, boy! Dammit, d'you think I'm offering you a plate of oysters?'

'No, sir, but—'

'But what?'

Now mere honesty compelled him to say what Sal had said, although then he had argued against her. 'I've no training in gentlemen's service—'

'What's training? *I* could train you. Devil take it, I've trained dogs and I've trained horses – surely I can train a lad with human understanding?'

'Of course, sir, but—'

'I know. You've a sweetheart – that pretty gal last night – she'd not let you go?'

Ben flushed. 'She's not my sweetheart, sir. We're friends, yes – she's a neighbour of ours – but there's nothing like that—'

'So – you've no ties?'

'Certainly not!'

'Then, confound it, what's holding you back? A young fellow like you – intelligent, well set-up, ambitious – don't deny it! The whole world open before you—'

'I know, sir—'

'Don't argue!' thundered Sir Henry.

Ben had no real desire to argue. He wanted desperately to be persuaded, and was only anxious that Sir Henry should not engage him because of a grateful impulse, and then regret it afterwards.

He left the hotel ten minutes later, having promised to consider the proposal. There was no immediate hurry, Sir Henry assured him. There would be many arrangements to make before he could leave on his tour. He had friends to consult and affairs to settle at his estate in Oxfordshire.

By the time Ben could tell Sal the result of the interview, before he left for the theatre that evening, he was more than half decided. His father thought it was a splendid opening.

His mother, more doubtful, said she must not stand in his way.

Sal's reactions were mixed. She was disappointed that Ben had been offered no instant cash reward, but excited by Sir Henry's proposal. 'It might lead anywhere,' she said.

'It would lead to Italy,' said Ben. 'That's what tempts me.'

'We'll miss you.' Sal's tears came easily. 'We'll *all* miss you. Me specially. But – I'd wait for you. If you wanted me to.'

Ben would have liked to say, 'Oh, there's no need for that,' but it would have sounded unkind. He could only pat her shoulder and mutter, 'I haven't gone yet. I don't know that I will.'

If Sal received his account with a few tears, old Linfoot received it with a gust of laughter next morning, as Ben undressed and donned the sandals of Perseus for the last time.

'And he said he wouldn't ask for testimonials, sir – as I was modelling for you. He says he knows you.'

'He does,' chuckled Linfoot, busily mixing his colours. 'And I know him.'

'It seems strange, sir – offering me a post in his service. I mean, I'm not trained as a footman or a valet or anything – I've never worked with horses, either. London must be full of experienced men wanting places—'

'It is, me boy, it is. Too many are seeking employment, these days.'

'So I don't understand why Sir Henry—'

'You will, me boy. You will.'

'Then why, sir?'

'He can't keep servants. His temper – they all know about him.' Linfoot let out another gust of laughter.

'Know what they call him? Horsewhip Harry!'

4 A ticket for tomorrow

'All the same, I perceive a new brightness in your eye this morning.' Linfoot applied another delicate dab of paint, giving to Perseus the liveliness that Ben was displaying for a quite different reason.

Ben dared not turn his head. Staring obediently in front of him, he spoke from the corner of his mouth. 'You're not – *warning* me – against Sir Henry?'

'What's the use of warning the young? They always know best.' Linfoot puffed out his cheeks, surveyed Ben critically, and stepped back from his canvas.

'All the same, sir, you think I'd be a fool to go?'

'You'd be a fool to refuse.'

'I thought you meant—'

Linfoot cut him short. 'You can look after yourself, I suppose? Strapping young fellow like you?'

'Ye-es—'

'You want to see Italy? Here's your chance. You *need* to visit Rome.'

'Need, sir?'

'To study the antique. Where it can be seen – in profusion – at its best.' Linfoot spoke jerkily between brush-strokes. 'I've looked through that portfolio of sketches you brought. You have a certain untaught talent. Pity you couldn't go through our Academy schools. But there – you have to earn your bread.'

'Indeed I have, sir.' Unwisely, Ben added, 'They say that Mr Turner never had any real training.'

Linfoot's howl of wrath almost blew him off the dais.

'Don't talk to me of Mr Turner! And don't go imitating him.'

'Er – no, sir.'

'Those sketches of yours – the morning mist on Hampstead Heath, the smoke over those cottage-chimneys at Paddington Green – oh, yes, and the lads bathing at Chelsea, with that terrible sunset – quite terrible, you must learn to do better than that! They all show the same thing – you're in danger – danger of infection – Mr Turner's manner—' Linfoot puffed like a scandalized grampus. 'The very last man to take as your model. No, me boy. What you want is discipline. A thorough grounding in the antique. So, as you can't go through the schools, take your chance and go to Italy.'

'I will, sir!' Ben clutched thankfully at the last remark. Here, at least, was something he could agree with.

'Turner!' Old Linfoot almost spat out the name. He stepped back a pace and gloated over the completed picture. 'They say he's showing a picture this year, *Dido and Aeneas*. Ha! We'll see which is the better – his or this *Perseus and Andromeda*. We'll see.' He began cleaning his brushes. 'You can get dressed, my boy. We'll have a glass of madeira before you go. I must wish you *bon voyage* – supposing Horsewhip Harry doesn't change his mind!'

Often, during the next few weeks, Ben felt that Sir Henry must indeed have changed his mind. No word came, though he had insisted on writing down Ben's address most particularly.

Still, he had said that there was no hurry. Grand folks of his kind had all manner of arrangements to make. Probably he did not want to miss the victory celebrations and the visit of the Allied sovereigns.

It was no moment to be out of London, the richest and gayest city in the world. For the time being, Ben forgot his restless urge to be off. There was so much happening all around him. And Sal – though he tried occasionally to give her the slip – demanded that he take her everywhere and escort her through the excited crowds. She was good enough company, but her tendency to treat him as her private property seemed to be increasing. Luckily she was often kept busy at the milliner's late into the evening, for all the ladies were ordering new bonnets at once.

Even so, they managed some outings together. They caught a glimpse of the Russian emperor, bowing from the balcony of his hotel in Piccadilly. They saw the grizzled old Prussian general, Blücher, drawn along in his carriage by delirious

Londoners who had taken the horses out of the shafts. They watched the guests stream into Carlton House for the Prince Regent's banquet. And on another evening they saw the emperor again, and a host of other resplendent notables, driving into the City to be welcomed by the Lord Mayor at Mansion House.

London that summer was all uniforms, jewels, medals, plumes and sashes, with bands blaring incessantly, church-bells pealing and fireworks hissing. There were hisses too for the portly, unpopular Prince Regent, when etiquette forced him to emerge and face the public. It was sad, thought Ben – while all these foreign war heroes were being cheered, Britain in the hour of her victory was headed by a prince so widely criticized. And he was there only because his poor old father was too sick in mind to carry out his kingly functions.

One thing Ben at first refused to do: when the Academy Exhibition opened, he would not take Sal to see Linfoot's painting.

'The Exhibition is not for the likes of us,' he told her. 'It's for the gentry.'

'Not after the first day or two, it isn't! It's open to all. You've only to look at the folk going in there.' He could not contradict her. Every time they passed along the Strand they could see the ordinary people filing in and out. 'I can pay for myself,' she taunted him.

'It isn't that, Sal—'

'I'd ha' thought Mr Linfoot could have given you a free pass or something. Being as you're in his picture.'

Ben did not like to say that this was the very reason for his reluctance. He wanted to see the other pictures – he would find far more interest in them than Sal would – but the idea of taking her to see *Perseus and Andromeda* filled him with alarm.

Eventually, because he was good-natured and she was obstinate, she had her way.

As he expected, she sailed briskly through the galleries, with only the briefest glance to left and right, until she found what she was looking for. Ben would have gladly lingered in front of Mr Turner's *Dido and Aeneas*. Sal marched him on.

Several ladies and gentlemen were ranged in front of Linfoot's canvas, discussing it in well-bred undertones. Ben quailed. He hastily detached himself from Sal's arm. If she wanted to gape at him dressed up – or rather undressed – as a Greek hero, he was not going to stand beside her. It was not likely that the other people would recognize him as the model, but Sal would say something to make sure that they did. He knew Sal.

He turned tail, and withdrew to the next room. There the girl pursued him five minutes later, pink and mischievous.

'Why did you run off like that? It's ever so nice. And they were saying ever such nice things – about *you*—'

'It's time we were going,' he said hastily, though they had only just come. In other circumstances he would gladly have spent an hour or two studying the pictures. But Sal's interest in painting was quickly satisfied, and, finding that she could not draw him back to that one exhibit, she was quite agreeable to leave.

She had been right about one thing. The picture found many admirers. Several other artists asked Linfoot the name of his male model. Ben found himself offered more work than he could have taken on, even in normal times. As it was, expecting a summons from Sir Henry any day, he felt he must refuse work that might last a long time. One could not suddenly desert a painter in the middle of an important composition.

Sal thought he was a fool. She said so. Working folk must look after themselves. Nobody else would. She was disgusted with the high-and-mighty Sir Henry. His promise was just a cock-and-bull story. As it would have meant Ben's leaving London, she was glad.

Ben still hoped. Sir Henry had spoken so definitely. Surely a gentleman like that would not break his word.

'You'll learn,' said Sal.

Certainly, as the weeks passed, the vision of Italy grew paler.

The foreign royalties departed. Fresh festivities began. It

was now the centenary of the House of Hanover, a hundred years since George I's arrival from Germany.

The royal parks were thrown open to all. St James's became a fairyland of coloured lanterns. Across the Mall, in Green Park, a sham citadel raised its temporary ramparts a hundred feet high and the storming of Badajoz was re-enacted with appropriate bangs and bugles. In Hyde Park whole fleets of miniature warships re-fought Nelson's Battle of the Nile on the waters of the Serpentine. And – a notable novelty – a balloon with passengers took off in front of Buckingham House.

After all this, the capital sank at last into its normal summer torpor. The people of quality departed, the theatres closed. Ben found himself completely unemployed, and at a time when discharged soldiers and sailors were streaming back in their thousands, all needing work.

Should he now go cap in hand to those artists whose offers he had previously refused? There was Mr Ruperts in Fitzroy Square. He'd been wanting models for some big Old Testament subject. Perhaps he could still use Ben for a morning or two.

Ben was just setting off to inquire when there was a knock on the door. Outside in the alley stood a supercilious young man, whom Ben guessed at first sight to be a lawyer's junior clerk.

'Are you Benjamin Reeth?'

'I am. Will you step inside?' Whatever the stranger's business, Ben knew his gossip-loving neighbours and preferred not to talk on the doorstep.

The clerk followed him disdainfully into the dark little parlour. 'We have received instructions from Sir Henry Hawthorn.'

'Sir Henry!' Ben's heart leaped.

'You are to join the establishment at Southampton.' The clerk handed over a letter. Ben felt the hardness of a coin through the folded paper. 'You will find here your coach-ticket and a guinea for any incidental expenses. On arrival, you will present yourself to Sir Henry at the Dolphin Inn.' Ben broke the seal and examined the contents with trembling fingers. 'I should like a receipt,' said the youth haughtily. 'If you can write your name, that is. Otherwise, your mark will suffice.'

Young cub, thought Ben. If he wants my *mark*, he'll have to make do with a black eye. But he merely answered, looking at the coach-ticket, 'I can write – and I can read too. You've bought me a ticket for tomorrow.'

'Of course.'

'Tomorrow! I don't know—'

'You don't know Sir Henry very well, perhaps?' suggested the clerk.

'No – that's true—'

'We do. We have acted for him ever since he inherited. You will learn that Sir Henry is a gentleman of swift decisions. When he is ready to go, he goes. If you wish to go with him—' The clerk paused with a significant shrug.

'All right,' said Ben. He found pen and ink, gave the required receipt, and showed his visitor to the door.

His parents seemed to accept this short notice as the most natural thing in the world. From childhood they had been taught that the gentry did not behave as humbler mortals did. They were born to wealth and power. God had arranged all that for the best. Lesser folk must spring gladly to do their bidding.

Sal was more rebellious. She thought that this sudden order, delivered by some whippersnapper of a lawyer's clerk, after so many weeks of silence, was utterly unreasonable. So, in his heart, did Ben. But as he wanted to obey it, he was not going to raise objections on principle.

Anyhow, by the time he broke the news to Sal that evening, the die was cast. His bag was packed with clean linen. His boots were polished like black glass. His mother had sponged and pressed his best coat. Whatever situation Sir Henry had in mind for him, it would presumably be 'all found', and Sir Henry would pay for whatever was needed. For his own amusement, Ben made space in his bag for a sketch-book and selection of pencils.

Just after six o'clock next morning he was on the top of the Southampton coach, bowling along through the outer suburbs at the start of his eighty-mile journey.

5 The establishment

Sir Henry looked even bigger than Ben remembered him. Squarely planted with his back to the afternoon sun, he filled the bow-window of the Dolphin.

'Ha! Here you are, my boy! Just in time.'

'I came at once, sir.' Ben had allowed himself only a few minutes to wash, change his necktie, and brush from his coat the dust collected in ten hours of summer driving. 'I received your message only yesterday morning.'

Sir Henry snorted. 'These confounded lawyers! Won't move themselves. Never mind. You're here now. We sail in the morning.' He turned to a lady seated near the window, sipping tea. 'This is the young fellow, Georgina. Ben Reeth.'

'Reeth but not wraith,' she said with a quick smile. She surveyed Ben from head to foot. 'A well set-up young man,' she said coolly. 'And very suitable to take on our foreign adventures.'

'So I thought, my dear. And not just for his muscles, eh, Ben – though we might be glad of them in a tight corner. He's artistic too.'

'He is, indeed, Harry.'

Ben did not care for the way the lady was assessing him. Standing there, silent and respectful, he had a chance to study her in turn. Youngish, strikingly beautiful, dressed in the very height of fashion, with much the same poise and considered gestures he had often admired in actresses from the wings . . . Something in her face, too, of the bold insolence that so often went with the ladies of the theatre . . .

'I mean,' Sir Henry explained, 'he's handy with a pencil. He can make sketches for us as we go. Anything we want to remember particularly – cathedrals, palaces, *you* know—'

'Yes, Harry, of course.' Rings flashed as her long white hand went up to screen a yawn. 'Well, if this captain of yours wishes us to sleep on board tonight—'

'He suggests it, my dear. We could sail on the morning tide.'

'I suppose it would save us from being dragged from our beds here at some ungodly hour. Very well.' She stood up reluctantly.

'Whatever you say.' Sir Henry, Ben noted, could be wonderfully tame.

The lady treated him to another long cool stare, then rustled from the room. Sir Henry followed, pausing only for a quick word. 'Find Jupp, my boy. He'll fix you up.' He strode out.

Puzzled, Ben went and inquired for Jupp.

'You mean the butler?' said a scurrying chambermaid. The whole inn was noisy with raised voices and flying footsteps and the bump of baggage.

'I suppose so—'

'Think he's in the yard—' She was gone.

Ben caught him as he was hurrying out under the archway: a plump, worried-looking little man, clutching a sheaf of papers. He swung round at Ben's voice. He had a pallid face, oval as an egg and just as smooth apart from wisps of black side-whisker.

'What is it? I can't stop now!'

'Sir Henry said I was to report to you.'

The butler's eyes narrowed. 'And who might you be?'

'My name's Reeth—'

'Ah!' The expression now was positively suspicious. 'Sir Henry told me.' He shuffled the lists in his hand. 'But I'm not quite clear about your position in the establishment.'

'Nor am I. I was sent for at a moment's notice—'

'That is Sir Henry's way.'

'But nothing's been settled,' said Ben urgently. 'Neither my duties nor my wages – nor how long we'll be away. And if we're leaving tomorrow—'

'Indeed we are.' Jupp groaned and brandished his papers. 'And I have to supervise that everything is safe aboard tonight. You had better come down to the pier with me. We can talk as we go. And you can help me with the checking of these lists.'

They set off down the High Street.

'You have not been in a gentleman's service before, I fancy?' The butler's manner continued faintly hostile.

'No. It's something quite fresh.'

'You will address me as "Mr Jupp". As Sir Henry's butler I am head of the establishment.'

'Yes, Mr Jupp.'

'The duration of the tour has not been decided. You will find that Sir Henry does not care to be tied down. He is a gentleman of – shall we say? – quick decisions.'

'So I have noticed! Mr Jupp.'

'As to wages, I cannot tell you until I have discussed the matter with Sir Henry. They will be fair, you may be sure.'

'I am sure they will be, Mr Jupp.' Ben was not unduly concerned. His chief desire was to get across the Channel.

'And all found, of course. Sir Henry is not a poor man. Nor a mean man. Whatever else can be said of him,' added the butler darkly. 'Your precise functions will have to be agreed later,' he went on. 'It would have been more usual if Sir Henry had informed me before engaging you.'

'He *is* a gentleman of quick decisions,' said Ben, stifling a smile. 'I'll be glad to make myself useful in any way, Mr Jupp. For instance, Sir Henry was saying to Lady Hawthorn—'

'That was *not* Lady Hawthorn.'

'Oh, I imagined . . .'

'You had best not imagine too much in this establishment. The simple truth is enough to be going on with. Lady Hawthorn decided against the tour. It was Lady Mulroy you must have seen. She is a great friend of Sir Henry's. So is Lord Mulroy.' The last remark sounded like an afterthought. 'They

34

are both coming on this jaunt. And that has caused half the trouble.'

'Trouble, Mr Jupp?'

'You could say "trouble",' the butler assured him with feeling. 'I am accustomed to the control of a large establishment. This is my first experience of – of a travelling circus!'

Ben thought he had better not echo each statement with a query. Time, no doubt, would explain everything. Meanwhile they had reached the harbour at the end of the street. His spirits rose.

Jupp led the way along the pier. They had to zigzag between mounds of merchandise and clusters of people.

'This is the vessel, I think.'

Ben saw a square-rigged two-master and read her name, the *Marigold*. He wondered if he dared ask where they were bound for. The butler would probably answer that he did not know, but that Sir Henry was a gentleman of unpredictable impulses, and that their destination might well be the Spanish Main. However, he risked a question, meekly and tentatively: 'Which French port are we making for, Mr Jupp?' He was half relieved, half disappointed, when the answer came, quite unremarkable: 'Rouen.'

'I'd imagined – I mean, I *expected* – that we'd be crossing by the ordinary packet—'

'Not with the size of *our* establishment. Sir Henry has been obliged to charter this vessel specially. One hundred and thirty pounds!' Ben gasped, as he was clearly expected to. 'They wanted a hundred and fifty,' the butler continued in a lower tone as they went up the gangway. 'He beat them down. Sir Henry has the money – but he knows what's fair.'

In the next two hours, standing at Jupp's elbow and checking off items as they were brought aboard, Ben gained a much clearer idea of the establishment which Jupp kept referring to with such reverence. It was no wonder that the recently resumed packet-boat had been judged inadequate.

Although their immediate concern was the safe stowing of the baggage, Ben was able during a slack moment to run his eye down the list of passengers. Besides Sir Henry and his guests there were Lady Mulroy's maid and his lordship's valet and coachman. Mr Jupp headed the establishment proper. There was Sir Henry's own valet, Marley. There was a cook, Mrs Tilberthwaite: it looked as though Sir Henry did not entirely trust the chefs of France to keep his body and soul together. There was a coachman. There was a second coachman. Two grooms. More surprisingly, there was a huntsman, then two men described as 'dog-feeders', and a falconer. After all these, hastily added in pencil, was 'B. Reeth', without any word of description.

The butler was in earnest consultation with the mate.

'Now the horses—'

'No problem. We've often shipped horses. The weather's set fair. It's only for a day and a night.'

'Ten horses, then. They'll be bringing them down presently. Some are very valuable animals.'

'Never fear. There's a proper way to handle them aboard ship. Dogs, now. We'll just have to shut them up. How many?'

'A hundred and five,' said Jupp.

'*What*?' cried the mate.

'Fifty couple of fox-hounds, a lap-dog of her ladyship's, and four gun-dogs for the gentlemen's shooting.'

'Why in Heaven's name do they want a pack of hounds?'

'You may well ask. Lord Mulroy is a very famous sporting man. And you know the winter we had this year – month after month of Arctic weather, all hunting stopped. So there we are – Lady Mulroy cannot go touring with Sir Henry unless his lordship comes with them, and Lord Mulroy will not be parted from his horses and hounds, so it is all or nothing. A circus,' said Mr Jupp venomously. 'Lord Mulroy cares for nothing with less than four legs.'

'Except his falcons?' suggested the mate with a rumbling laugh.

'Yes. You must find somewhere to stow those infernal birds.'

Further conversation was interrupted as another carriage came clattering along the pier, piled high with baggage.

There were – Ben never forgot the number as long as he lived – precisely one hundred and seventeen listed boxes, trunks, bundles and other items, with a separate sheet enumerating the twenty-eight firearms, ranging from fowling-pieces to duelling-pistols, judged indispensable to the enjoyment of a Continental tour.

He was relieved to see his own bag safely brought down from the Dolphin. He saw it stowed in the cramped sleeping-quarters he was to share with the other men-servants, and then hurried back to the butler's side.

He had certainly been dropped straight into this job, he reflected wryly. There had not been a moment yet for a bite of food. There would be supper, he assumed, when loading was complete. Meanwhile, used as he was to working under pressure at the theatre, he did not complain.

He was the only person who was not doing so.

As he began to identify the other members of the establishment, one by one, he was aware of an undercurrent of rebellion. There were sour faces and sulks. When he carried his bag below, the two grooms were conferring in furious whispers, which ceased as he greeted them. They answered him glumly. As he left, one muttered to the other, 'Best not – he mayn't stand in with us.'

The chief grumbler seemed to be the valet, a dandified young man with a would-be genteel voice. He came up to the butler and launched into a string of grievances about the accommodation.

Jupp waved him away testily. 'You'll have to make do, Marley—'

'It's not good enough, Mr Jupp!'

'It's good enough for this short time.'

'It's all the other things. We've asked and asked, and we've had no proper answers. I've been talking to the other servants—'

'I am sure you have,' said the butler meaningly. 'Just be patient a little longer – I must choose my moment with Sir Henry. Leave it for now, Marley. Here comes Russell.'

It was not only Russell, the huntsman, who was approaching the foot of the gangway. Watched by a crowd of fascinated townsmen, his pack of hounds came flowing along the quay, a compact rippling mass of white and tan and black, a hundred keen heads lifting or dropping to snuffle over the cobbles with their unfamiliar scents.

'See what you meant by circus,' said the ship's mate.

With surprisingly little fuss the huntsman got them all aboard, with the help of his two dog-feeders, and down into a straw-strewn quarter of the hold allotted to them.

'At least we needn't count *them*,' said Jupp with relief. 'Russell knows every one by name.'

At last there was a lull. Everything on the lists was checked off except Lady Mulroy's barouche, for which a space had been reserved on the deck. This, Ben gathered, was a most particular vehicle. Although Sir Henry was taking his own travelling carriage, already hoisted aboard and firmly roped down, Lady Mulroy had declined to venture on the roads of Europe without it.

'Double springs,' said Jupp respectfully. 'Pillows and cushions – all finest eiderdown – so she can sleep if she wants to. Like an elegant little bedroom almost. There's a bookcase, a writing desk, everything a lady could wish for.'

Lady Mulroy was so devoted to her barouche that she required it even for the final quarter-mile journey from the inn. It must be loaded last, no matter with what inconvenience, and secured against damage from weather or the motion of the ship.

At least there would be no more horses to coax aboard. They were taking only hunters. For the barouche and the other two carriages they would hire as they went.

While Sir Henry and his friends lingered at the Dolphin, there was time to snatch a meal below-decks. Jupp took the head of the table and made sure that he was served first, but he could hardly be said to preside. The Mulroys' Irish maid and valet kept to themselves. The Mulroy coachman would arrive with the barouche. Sir Henry's servants clustered round the valet at the far end, conferring in undertones. Ben sat alone, uneasily conscious of their stares. How would this adventure turn out? It was understandable that these flunkeys should view him coldly until they knew him better. He did not belong to their world. Well, it was too late to turn back.

A shout from the deck gave warning that the barouche had been sighted. Jupp rose. 'Come along, all of you. We must be there to receive Sir Henry.'

'We'll be there,' said one of the grooms. There was some laughter as they pushed their way out.

The barouche made an impressive sight as it came along the pier, the cockaded driver majestic on his high box, the Mulroy crest on the door-panel flashing golden in the sunset.

'There's no space here,' said Jupp pettishly. 'We had better line up on the quay.'

'That will suit perfectly,' said the valet. His tone puzzled Ben but there was no time for speculation. He followed the others as they filed down the gangway and fell into line.

The barouche came to a standstill. One of the grooms sprang forward, opened the door with a flourish, and let down the steps. A dainty slipper appeared, then an immense bonnet framing Lady Mulroy's deceptively delicate features, and finally the whole of that slender lady, a white high-waisted divinity, draped in a golden shawl that dazzled the dying sun itself.

Ben had already heard the servants refer to her as 'the gorgeous Georgina' and now he fully understood why. Her effect upon the sailors lining the bulwarks was audible, but respectfully muted. The loungers on the pier were free to express their admiration more loudly. They did so.

Equally open was their ribald amusement when her lady-ship was followed by her husband. It was Ben's first glimpse of the sport-loving nobleman. He made a grotesque picture, like some caricature by Gillray. Though (as Ben learned later) he was only a few years older than Lady Mulroy, he could have been her father. A life of hard riding and fearless jumping had left him with bandy legs and a broken nose. He had obviously been drinking heavily. He waddled a few paces after his wife and then stopped, peering at the ship as though it were an unexpected obstruction.

Sir Henry got out last, flushed and jovial. The butler stepped forward.

'All ready, Jupp?'

'Yes, Sir Henry. Just the barouche, sir, then we'll be all ready to sail tomorrow morning.'

'Beg your pardon, Sir Henry—' It was the valet, suddenly taking the stage. 'That isn't quite right. Whatever Mr Jupp says, we are *not* ready to sail.'

Ben would never have believed that Sir Henry's face could go any redder. It did.

'What the devil do you mean, Marley? What's this?'

The valet was thrusting forward a paper.

'We're standing together, Sir Henry. These are our demands—'

'Demands? Have you gone mad? Talking like a confounded Jacobin – an infernal revolutionary—'

'Read it, Sir Henry.' There was a rumble of support from the other Hawthorn servants. They broke line and clustered together as if to give each other courage.

Their master held the paper at arm's length. His pale eyes bulged with incredulous fury.

'What's this nonsense? An advance in wages? Written agreements? Guaranteed passages home if dismissed? Never heard such nonsense in all my life!'

'Oh, yes, you have, sir. We've mentioned the matter more than once.'

'Then you'll not mention it again.' Sir Henry ripped the paper across, and again, and let the evening breeze carry the pieces into the water on the far side of the pier. 'You can go to the devil,' he roared. 'Or go to my cabin! Get on with your proper duties.'

Marley did not budge. Encouraged by the murmur behind him, he shouted back: 'Oh, no, Sir Henry! If you won't grant our demands, we're not going. Any of us. And that's flat.' He turned to the others. 'I'm speaking for all of you a'n't I?'

'That's right!' The chorus was ragged but seemed unanimous.

'So you see, sir,' cried Marley, elated. 'We're all in this together. Either you do the right thing—'

'I'll do the right thing!'

Sir Henry's promise came like a howl of frenzy. Snatching the coachman's whip, he lashed out. The valet skipped back and the end of the whip merely flicked his ankles. Sir Henry marched slowly after him, stride after majestic stride, the whip cracking again and again like a succession of pistol-shots. Marley was driven back, squealing in protest, his hands fluttering helplessly.

'You'd stir up a mutiny, would you? Rabble-rousing Radical! Agitator! Is this what they term a "strike", then? I'll show you how to strike!' The whip cracked terrifyingly and the valet cried again for mercy, though the lash had barely touched him. Sir Henry was an artist with that whip. He might be bellowing like a maniac, but he was completely in control.

Marley retreated before him. Several of the spectators yelled a warning as he neared the edge of the pier. Sir Henry pressed on relentlessly. For an agonizing moment the valet was silhouetted like a capering marionette against the sunset. Then he was gone, with one last despairing screech. There was a heavy splash from below. A fan of water sprayed up and spattered the cobbles.

Sir Henry peered down into the harbour. He laughed gustily. 'Fish him out by all means,' he called to the boatmen who rushed to the rescue. 'But don't expect any reward.' He swung round and faced the rest of the servants. 'Any one else taking a bath?' No one answered. 'Then get aboard, the lot of you!' There was only the briefest hesitation. The men glanced at each other, and at the bedraggled, spluttering Marley as he reappeared, clambering up a ladder. Then with one accord they turned and filed obediently up the gangway.

Ben was not sure whether the order included himself. He took his cue from the butler, who remained where he was, deferentially waiting for his master to go first.

'Put that ruffian's bag ashore, Jupp. He's dismissed.'

'Very good, Sir Henry.'

Lady Mulroy had been much diverted by the whole spectacle. 'But, my dear Harry! How can you go without a valet?'

Sir Henry's face broke into an immense grin, his good humour entirely restored. He slapped a hand on Ben's shoulder. It was like the well-meaning tap of a lion's paw. 'This young fellow will do me well enough.' And addressing Ben he said with great self-satisfaction: 'And it settles the problem of what to do with *you*. So *everybody's* happy!'

Ben wondered.

6 All at sea

What exactly, wondered Ben, was expected of a valet?

The other servants showed no willingness to help the man who had just replaced their spokesman. Even Jupp clearly disapproved of an untrained outsider's appointment to this privileged post. Lord Mulroy's valet, Doyle, was openly disgusted. When Ben appealed to him, the sandy-haired Irishman looked down his long nose and contrived to answer volubly without giving any useful information away.

'A valet's duties can't be summed up in a few words. Nor learned in a few days. It takes years, and in the best houses, town and country, every manner of social occasion.'

'I'm sure it does.'

'No one can tell a valet what is proper. He should know. It's *he* must tell his master – tactfully, mind – if the necessity should arise. He can't *say* what his gentleman ought to wear, he has to guide him by laying out the right clothes.'

'I see,' said Ben, growing more and more alarmed.

'Of course,' said Doyle in a superior tone, 'working for a country squire like Sir Henry, who's no more than a baronet, ye'll not meet all the finer problems ye would in the service of the nobility. Ye'll not have to find ye way round the backstairs at Windsor or Dublin Castle—'

'Well, hardly,' said Ben gently, 'as we are going in the opposite direction.'

Doyle scowled, but the Hawthorn servants seemed to appreciate this retort. Already they were resenting the Irishman's manner.

Ben was learning fast, picking up crumbs of information from the talk around him. Sir Henry might be 'a mere baronet' with only four thousand acres, whereas Lord Mulroy was a viscount with forty thousand, but those vaster estates consisted mainly of peat-bog, while Sir Henry's were fertile farmland in the English Midlands and, better still, profitable coalfields in Durham.

Sir Henry, in short, was the man with the money. His lordship was deep in debt. It had suited him nicely to come on this tour abroad with a friend to pay the expenses.

Fortunately for Ben, that first night, not much could be expected of any valet with only the limited facilities of the *Marigold* available.

He checked that Sir Henry's bunk was prepared with clean sheets and pillow. He rummaged carefully in his master's baggage until he came upon nightcap, slippers, and a nightshirt as voluminous as a tent. He laid out toilet requisites, a fresh shirt for the morrow, and an immaculate stock to be neatly knotted round those fleshy folds of jaw. Apart from some energetic work with clothes-brush and boot-polish, he could think of nothing else to do.

Very soon, no doubt, Sir Henry would give further instructions.

Doyle, he noted, had not yet retired. He was seated on a hatch, staring at the lighted windows of the town, swigging frequently from a flask. Ben caught the whiff of Irish whiskey on the warm air.

He had better take his cue from Doyle: a valet saw his master to bed before turning in. He wondered how much longer their employers would remain drinking with the captain. As if in answer to his speculation, he heard a burst of feminine laughter, and Lady Mulroy emerged, supported on Sir Henry's arm. She saw Doyle and called to him imperiously.

'His lordship is ready for bed. More than ready. He will need your assistance to undress.'

'At once, my lady!' Doyle hurried below.

Sir Henry was peering into the shadows. 'That you, Reeth?'

'Yes, sir!'

'Off to bed with you, my boy. I'll not require you any more tonight. You've had a hard day. Get some sleep.'

'Thank you, sir. Good-night, sir. Good-night, my lady.'

Ben went thankfully below, leaving them to promenade the deck in the lantern-light. But the much-needed sleep came slowly, and brought bizarre dreams.

From these he was roused eventually by the rumble of feet overhead and the shouting of orders. The porthole had changed to a pale disc of early daylight. The whole feel of the ship had changed. She was no longer shifting gently at her moorings. She was moving, but now with direction and purpose.

Doyle and the other men were still huddled in their bunks, heavily asleep. Ben pushed back the blanket, dropped softly and pulled on his clothes. Then he went on deck into the golden glory of the dawn.

The *Marigold* was gliding down the estuary under a good spread of canvas. The town was already a faint blur, far astern. Ahead, the green jaws of the land opened to the sparkling expanse of the Solent. It must be the Isle of Wight beyond, pearly in the haze, seeming almost to float on the surface of the water.

A superb morning. Watercolour would have been the thing. He screwed up his eyes, composing pictures. He tried to imagine what Mr Turner would have done with this entrancing blend of land and sea, sunray and cloud. Suddenly, as he leant over the rail, he became aware of another cloud looming over him.

44

'Oh – good morning, Sir Henry!' He sprang erect. 'I thought it best not to disturb you. I didn't realize—'

'Quite all right, my boy.' Sir Henry looked round him, snuffing the fresh air like a benign bull. 'Can't stand fellows fussing over me at all hours. Lot of confounded nonsense. Worse still in that box of a cabin. Positive hell-hole! I can put on my own breeches. Old enough – ain't I?'

'Of course, sir.' Ben thought he had better get things straight from the start. 'But, sir, I must depend upon you to tell me my duties.'

'Depend on it, I will!' Sir Henry chuckled alarmingly. 'Just now, all I want is a shave.'

'Er – yes, sir.'

'Get some hot water. From the cook's galley or whatever they call it.'

'At once, sir!'

In a few minutes Ben presented himself in the cabin with a steaming can. Sir Henry fixed him with a shrewd look, divining his nervousness. 'Ha! Ever shaved another man?'

'Only my father, once or twice,' Ben admitted, 'when he was ill.'

'Then I'll be hanged if you practise on *me*! Tuck that towel round me. You can work up the lather and wield the brush – suit your artistic talents!' Sir Henry roared good-humouredly and sat down on the edge of his bunk. 'I'll handle the razor myself.'

'As you wish, sir.' Ben felt vastly relieved. The vessel was beginning to roll slightly as it reached more open water.

'That last fellow – damned rogue – reckoned no gentleman should shave himself. Infernal poppycock! Am I a man – or a barber's dummy? Hey?'

'Very much a man, I should say, sir.'

The flashing steel rasped across Sir Henry' jowl, to and fro, to and fro, before moving up to chin and cheek. Ben, standing patiently in attendance with another towel and the sheets of thin paper on which to wipe the blade, was vividly reminded of some red-brown winter field reappearing, furrow by furrow, as the snow melted.

'I've no patience with this Beau Brummell flummery.' Sir Henry screwed up his features to execute some delicate work on his long upper lip. 'There,' he concluded, passing the razor to Ben for its final wipe, 'that's it. Without a drop of innocent blood shed. Which is more than that devil Boney could ever claim.' He leapt up, tearing the towel from his shoulders and dabbing his face.

Bonaparte and Beau Brummell were apparently the two main objects of Sir Henry's dislike.

Ben could understand the reason for the first. The second was explained to him later by Jupp. It seemed that once, in a public place, the famous dandy had made a disparaging remark about the cut of Sir Henry's waistcoat. Having no horsewhip handy – they were at a ball at Charnwood House – Sir Henry had proposed lifting Brummell by his exquisitely-tied stock and, after a period of dangling in mid-air, dropping him from the balcony into Piccadilly. Only the presence of Brummell's particular friend, the Prince Regent, had frustrated this plan.

In consequence, Sir Henry had been left with a brooding contempt for the Beau, and for all those who meekly followed his social lead. Ben had good cause to be thankful for the incident. Sir Henry had reacted so violently that he now had no use for fashion – and precious little for a valet, though he still employed one from force of habit. He scorned fuss and liked to be independent. So long as someone laid out clean linen and kept his boots shining, he could look after himself.

There was scarcely any more required of Ben that first day. He unpacked his sketchbook and chose a shady corner on the deck from which he could observe his surroundings and the company.

It was a perfect day for the crossing. Even out in the open Channel the water was barely ruffled. The vessel glided southwards under full canvas with only the slightest roll. Lord Mulroy paid several anxious visits to his horses, below decks, but emerged each time to assure his wife that all was well. The gorgeous Georgina, enthroned like some northern Cleopatra upon a mound of carriage-cushions, with an immense hat to protect her renowned complexion from the sun, and long white gloves to preserve her hands, did not seem unduly concerned. She was absorbed in Lord Byron's recent poem, *The Corsair*.

Sir Henry, when not dancing attendance upon his guest, stalked the deck with a morose expression, as though, after the first few hours at sea, he was finding the inactivity irksome.

Once he called to Cripps, the falconer, 'How about having the birds out, hey? Try them after a seagull, hey?'

Cripps thought this would not answer. It might not be a good idea at all. His falcons were not accustomed to seagulls. He did not fancy risking them over the open sea.

'All right,' said Sir Henry sourly. 'Have it your own way.'

He cheered up when he paused beside Ben and examined his sketches. Ben had been interested in the elaborate patterning overhead – the sharp lines of the rigging, the swelling curves of sailcloth – but he had also attempted, without great success, to catch the sailors as they fell into the natural poses of their work. There was such life in those tough bodies, such character in the weather-beaten faces. But he was baffled by his lack of skill. His hand could not come near the image that his eye saw.

Sir Henry was less critical. 'Not bad, my boy. Not bad at all.'

Lord Mulroy waddled over. 'H'm. Ever draw horses?'

'I've never tried, my lord.'

'Pity.' The viscount gave up the idea with obvious regret. 'Picture of a good horse – a real thoroughbred – always worth having.' He turned to Sir Henry. 'Remember that hunter of mine? Black Turk? Got an artist fellow to paint him. Oils. Big picture. Cost me a hundred guineas. I say "cost me"—' he laughed croakily. 'I *meant* to pay. I swear I did. Never had a chance, though. Three years after he'd finished it, fellow died. Must show it you sometime, Harry. Before the bailiffs get it.' He lurched away across the deck, his interest in art exhausted.

Sir Henry's, however, was not. Soon he beckoned Ben over to where Lady Mulroy was reclining. She looked up from her book with as much of a welcoming smile as Ben's lowly position rated.

'Well, Reeth, Sir Henry thinks you should take my likeness.'

Ben stood aghast. 'You must excuse me, my lady. I'm not competent.'

'Oh, come, come – Sir Henry says you have a gift.'

'I daren't attempt a portrait, my lady. I can't really draw people at all yet. Mr Linfoot says I ought to study anatomy—'

'No time like the present, hey, Georgina?' interrupted Sir Henry with gusto. 'Could hardly do better.' Lady Mulroy gave him a reproving glance that wiped the leer from his face.

'And for another thing,' Ben went on hurriedly, 'he thinks I should make a thorough study of the antique—'

'Well, I am hardly *that*,' said her ladyship emphatically, 'whatever other appeal I may possess for the artist. Never mind, Reeth. You may try. What else is there to do on this monotonous voyage?' She dropped her eyes to the volume of Byron again, turning her head artlessly to present her famous profile.

Profiles were at least easier than the half-turned face. Ben did his best. The brow, the imperious nose, and the lush mouth came easily enough. The hair was not too difficult, especially the elaborately-styled corkscrew curls arranged on the cheek, but no mere pencil could do justice to its colour. Feeling that a little flattery might be prudent, Ben endowed her ladyship with rather more chin than nature had provided.

'Capital!' cried Sir Henry – too impulsively, as it proved.

Lady Mulroy's opinion was quite different. 'He's made me look like a hag!' she exclaimed. She ripped the sheet from the sketchbook and crumpled it angrily. 'You were quite right, Reeth – you should not attempt portraits. When we get to the Roman ruins, you may do very well.'

Ben retired with as much dignity as he could. After that, he kept well out of her sight. The story ran round the establishment and there was a good deal of sniggering at his expense.

The favouring breeze held steady. At sunset the coast of Normandy drew a firm dark line between sea and sky. Sir

Henry surveyed it exultantly, like a victorious commander about to invade.

'Boney!' he said. 'I'd like to see his face.'

Sir Henry, Ben had already realized, considered himself a simple British patriot with the soundest possible views upon the world. Germans and Russians, Spaniards and Portuguese, were foreigners; tiresome but with the one redeeming feature that they had fought against Napoleon. The French had got rid of Boney at last, but he would not trust them a yard. They produced excellent brandy and champagne. Otherwise, Sir Henry could not imagine what God had been about when he created the French.

Ben had absorbed rather different ideas from listening to old Linfoot, but he knew it was wiser to keep them to himself.

Dawn found the *Marigold* gliding between two green arms of land, with lengths of chalk cliff. They were approaching the mouth of the Seine. Coming into view on the port side was Le Havre.

At breakfast there was a furious argument between Sir Henry and the captain, clearly audible to Ben as he sat on a hatch not far from the cabin-door.

'Our agreement was for Rouen!'

'I'm sorry, Sir Henry, you must have misunderstood—'

'I did *not* misunderstand. You said Rouen.'

'I could not possibly. The *Marigold* draws too much water to sail so far up-river.'

'*Are you calling me a liar?*'

'No, sir, I am merely telling you that I must put you ashore at Le Havre.'

The conversation grew more and more heated. Sir Henry told the captain that he was not fit to command a canal-boat. The captain retorted that never again would he demean his fine vessel by turning it into a Noah's Ark.

By this time the *Marigold* was swinging to port and nosing her way into the harbour. The captain gladly seized the excuse to break off the discussion so that he could supervise the berthing of his ship.

The next few hours were extremely tedious for everyone

but Sir Henry, who clearly enjoyed nothing so much as a really passionate dispute, especially one with legal complications.

The ship lay at the quayside. Only the captain went ashore, and then only to fetch certain officials. Not a bag was landed. The French dockers lounged in the midday sun, staring with puzzled and increasingly sullen faces.

Sir Henry was finally persuaded that, whatever promises had been understood, the *Marigold* was physically incapable of going up the Seine as far as Rouen. He could land here at Le Havre or he could return to England.

When Sir Henry decided to make the best of it, and disembark, the captain insisted upon payment before the hatches were taken off. And not a single passenger was going to set foot on shore.

'And who's going to stop *me* from going ashore?' demanded Sir Henry, looking round for a horsewhip.

The port officials interrupted soothingly to assure him that no one would actually bar his passage. But, if he did not pay the captain the sum agreed, they would be bound to hold his horses and carriages as security for the money.

After another half-hour of shouting they came to a compromise. For conveying the establishment only as far as Le Havre, the captain would reduce the cost by thirty pounds. Sir Henry paid up good-temperedly, confident that he had won, and swaggered triumphantly down the gangway.

It took the rest of that afternoon to disembark the party, horse, hound and falcon, not to mention the gorgeous Georgina. In Le Havre a rumour spread that the Prince Regent of England had landed with his current lady-love.

7 Confounded foreigners

At Justien's Hotel the confusion was indescribable.

Sir Henry did not help matters. He assumed that all foreigners could understand English if it was bellowed at them with sufficient emphasis.

Lady Mulroy alone attempted to speak French, and she used it only for her personal requirements. She quickly secured a bowl of water for her lap-dog, but the hotel seemed absurdly ill-prepared for the accommodation of a hundred fox-hounds.

Monsieur Justien ran to and fro, clicking his fingers and exclaiming '*Mon dieu!*' More and more luggage piled up in the entrance. When it was drawn to the notice of scurrying servants, they stared, shrugged and vanished. Ben had to carry Sir Henry's bags upstairs himself.

In his innocence he had expected these people to greet the English as liberators. Had not Britain delivered the hapless French from a quarter-century nightmare of revolution and terror, dictatorship and war?

The hotel servants seemed unaware of this. They were not noticeably pleased to see English faces, except for that of King George III on the coins dropped into their ready palms.

Sir Henry was fuming like a volcano on the verge of eruption. 'Upon my soul, I think these confounded foreigners are all mad! And damnably impertinent. You would think that *they* had won the war.'

At that moment, most happily, Pierre Arnauld made his appearance. Suddenly he was there, seemingly from nowhere, a bright-eyed thirtyish fellow, handsome but for the grey sabre-scar across his brown cheek, and with one of those curling moustaches that every other Frenchman seemed to wear.

'You are perhaps in need of a courier, milord?'

Finding himself addressed in English, and as 'milord', Sir Henry relaxed visibly.

'Am I, indeed?'

'It is usual, milord. To save you from — what do you call them? — the troublesome details that pettifog?' White teeth flashed under the black moustache. The young man bowed and held out some papers. 'Permit me! My testimonials. Naturally, there has not been time yet to win many.'

Sir Henry peered. 'H'm. So this Doctor Murray found you "most trustworthy and conscientious" . . . And who's this one from? The Governor of Dartmoor Prison?'

'I have been prisoner of war, milord. A hussar. Taken by your great General Wellington in Spain.'

'The devil you were!' Sir Henry bristled, remembered that the war was over, and became genial again. 'H'm. Governor says you were "a model prisoner". Applied yourself to learning English. Very helpful in dealing with the other prisoners.' Suddenly Sir Henry's vast waistcoat began to heave with silent laughter. 'He says you "displayed exceptional artistic skill" — in "carving small objects out of *meat-bones*"! Now that's a qualification,' said Sir Henry with ponderous sarcasm, 'I should find of the greatest practical utility. Just the kind of fellow I'm looking for!'

The former hussar stood his ground with good-humoured dignity. 'Many of us amused ourselves in this manner, milord. It passed the time. And we could sell our carvings, through the guards, for a little pocket-money. We had no materials but the bones left on our dinner-plates.'

'Very resourceful! I like that.' Sir Henry handed back the testimonials. 'I'll give you a trial. Can't manage in this benighted country without someone who understands the lingo. But by gad — if you cheat me, I'll break every bone in your body! And you can amuse yourself carving them!'

'Thank you, milord. You will have no occasion.'

Once Pierre took charge there was an instant transformation. In no time Sir Henry and the Mulroys were sitting down to a dinner which even Jupp, hovering anxiously behind their chairs, could not fault in any way. Later, the humbler members of the party were served in their turn. Some grumbled at the frenchified dishes, but Ben thoroughly enjoyed his first omelette, the fresh-caught fish in its highly-flavoured sauce, the piled-up basket of fruit straight from the Norman orchards, and the rough red wine in its earthenware pitcher. No doubt of it, he was abroad at last.

He felt that even more when, before bed, he took a turn through the streets. Vibrant voices rang through the September darkness, and not a word could he understand. Hanging lanterns glimmered on outlandish names and incomprehensible announcements. The smells from the doorways, the rough paving underfoot, the style of the window-shutters, the very pitch of the roofs – all were provokingly unfamiliar.

He must, he resolved, learn some of what Sir Henry termed 'the lingo'. If Pierre could master English so well, surely he could acquire at least a little French – if only a few phrases for dealing with waiters and chambermaids? If he knew 'hot' and 'cold', 'clean' and 'dirty', 'look sharp about it' and 'this won't do', he would be much better equipped for his post as valet.

There were still plenty of people about. The men were smallish, though their military moustaches gave them an aggressive air. The girls tripped along with a lively step, close caps framing their round faces. Their earrings and necklaces and crucifixes sparkled in the lamplight – but nothing sparkled more than their mischievous eyes. They stared and giggled, no doubt because of his height and English appearance. *'Grisettes'* he soon learned to call these attractive working-girls, so much a feature of every French town. It was one of the first words Pierre taught him.

Soon he found himself back at the waterfront. The harbour glistened black, with yellow reflections wobbling. A tipsy sailor came staggering from a tavern. He was singing at the top of his voice. Even sung like that, slurred and jerky, the song kept some of its swing and splendour. Ben had heard it in London, chanted by rioting radicals to annoy the authorities. He knew it was the marching song of the French Revolution. It had taken Napoleon's armies to the ends of Europe, from Portugal to Russia. It was the Marseillaise.

'Marchons! Marchons—'

Two anxious shipmates caught up with the sailor and tried to shush him. He defied them. They clapped a hand over his mouth. They all three lurched to and fro, perilously near the edge of the quay. Then suddenly the drunk man gave in, good-humouredly, and they released him. They walked away amicably arm in arm, changing the song.

'*Auprès de ma blonde,*
Qu'il fait bon dormir!'

Staring after them, Ben was suddenly aware of some one behind him. He spun round, and was relieved to recognize the courier.

'You should take care – in these streets – an Englishman.' Pierre spoke softly and pleasantly, but there was no doubt about the warning in his voice.

'Thank you. I suppose one should always be careful in sea-ports. There are parts of London, near the docks . . . But I can look after myself.'

'I can believe that. None the less, take care. It has been a long war with England. Not everyone forgets quickly.'

Pierre seemed anxious to walk back to the inn with him, and Ben was glad enough of his company. The courier explained the meaning of the little scene he had just witnessed.

'The Marseillaise is now forbidden here. The tricolour also. Only the plain white cockade of King Louis is permitted to be worn in the hat – the red-white-and-blue cockade is banned. Once more the flag must be the three golden lilies on blue.'

Pierre spoke evenly. Ben could not see his face. None the less, he sensed powerful emotion beneath that calm exterior. Pierre, he guessed, had no enthusiasm for the restored Louis. At heart, he was still the hussar who had ridden to battle behind the eagle standards of Napoleon.

Well, it was all over and done with, now.

The next morning, Sir Henry demanded his hunting-coat. Ben had by this time acquired a working knowledge of his master's wardrobe, and the scarlet coat was quickly brushed and laid out.

'Too early in the season, by rights. Might kill a cub or two. Horses need exercise, anyhow.' Sir Henry chuckled and the razor trembled perilously. 'His lordship's in a mood to chase anything. One of these Frenchies, if all else fails.'

It was a fine crisp morning. Lord Mulroy was pacing the inn-yard, eager to be off. But the departure of so large a party took some organizing. Pierre seemed equal to every problem.

Even Sir Henry agreed that there must be a plan, with an overnight stop at Bolbec, halfway to Rouen. The carriages would take the high road and Pierre would hurry ahead to reserve the accommodation. The two gentlemen would make their own way there, with their full retinue of huntsmen, grooms and falconer, finding what sport they could. With the hills on their left, and the Seine on their right, they could scarcely lose themselves.

'Capital,' said Henry. 'I feel like a gallop.'

He was destined to disappointment. Lady Mulroy came down at last, exquisitely attired for travelling in a long green pelisse, with her maid close behind, arms full of the dribbling dog.

The proposed arrangement did not suit her ladyship. 'So *I* am to sit for hours alone in the barouche, bored to distraction? And with no one to protect me? In an enemy country?'

'Oh, come, Georgina,' said Sir Henry, 'hardly an enemy country now. And you won't lack protection – dash it, three carriages! There'll be Jupp—'

'Jupp! Much protection he would be!'

'Doyle, then – and young Ben here—'

'Ben is another matter,' Lady Mulroy admitted grudgingly. Ben, waiting dutifully in the background, felt himself flush. 'But he cannot protect me from *boredom* if he is sitting in the second carriage fifty yards behind! I like conversation, Harry. I did not accept your invitation to this tour – a most pressing invitation – just to jog along foreign roads by myself, while you go galloping over the fields with Humphy.'

Sir Henry's cheeks were hotter than Ben's. 'Just as you wish!' His tone was almost curt. He went to the door and bawled to one of the grooms. 'I shall not want Grey Bark after

all! No! I shall not be riding today. I am going in the barouche.'

'That will be delightful,' said Lady Mulroy triumphantly.

Ben certainly found that drive delightful, whatever the atmosphere was like in the barouche bowling along ahead.
Neither Jupp nor Doyle said much to him, and he was free to
study the changing scene that unfolded outside the carriage-
window.

France, or this part at least, did not look so different from
England. Much the same oaks and beeches were beginning to
flaunt their autumn glory. The glistening Seine, sighted at
intervals, might have been the Thames.

To an observant eye, though, there were variations. The
style of the new-looking villas, the garb of the peasants toiling
in field and orchard, even the way the hayricks had been built
. . . such details, and a host of others, he itched to pin down in
his sketchbook.

The road was remarkably good. Old Linfoot had told such
dismal stories of the continental roads over which he had been
rattled in the days of his youth. Bonaparte, however, with all
his faults, had made great improvements. 'But of course!'
Pierre explained to Ben that evening. 'He gave us straight
roads and better surfaces – and shade. Only a year or two ago
he made a fresh order: wherever there was a road without
trees, they must be planted along the side. And wait until you
cross the Alps! If your master travels on to Italy—'

'He has promised that he will,' said Ben quickly.

'Then you will see how the Emperor set his engineers to
blast roads through the mountains. Never before were there
such roads.'

They had two changes of horses on their way. But Pierre,
riding fast in front of them, had paused at each posting station
to give warning of the English party. The others had the fresh
beasts ready, and the unharnessing was accomplished before
even Sir Henry could show impatience. By early afternoon
they were at Bolbec, and there was the courier smiling from
the doorway of the Hotel de la Poste, with the innkeeper and a
posse of servants in attendance.

'Dinner can be served whenever milady desires. Or would she prefer to wait for milord?'

'No use waiting for him,' said Lady Mulroy decisively. 'If he's found something to chase, he'll go on till sunset. Give us time to remove the dust. Sir Henry and I will dine at three.'

Lord Mulroy arrived when the meal was half over, and went straight to the table, though Ben overheard his wife complaining that he was mud-spattered and sweaty. His lordship ignored this, announcing that he was as hungry as a hunter.

'What else *are* you? I declare you take away my appetite. You bring the stench of the stables into the dining-room.'

Sir Henry broke in tactfully, anxious to keep the peace. 'Had a good day, Humphrey? What d'ye think of the country?'

'Not bad, not bad. Fences put me in mind of Ireland. High banks, broad too, well-planted with hedges. Need to watch where you jump. Very sporting, though.'

His lordship fell noisily upon his soup. So far as Ben could hear, he found nothing more to say about the landscape of Normandy.

The next day, Lord Mulroy insisted that Sir Henry ride with him. Her ladyship glowered, Sir Henry wavered, but eventually – with insincere apologies to her – did what he most wanted to do.

It was perhaps as well. Even she admitted that when they rejoined her at the hotel in Rouen. In his sporting enthusiasm Lord Mulroy had charged hell-for-leather across country, scattering the livestock in all directions. Eventually he had been cornered by a group of infuriated peasants, brandishing sharp implements. Only the arrival of Sir Henry had persuaded them to release his lordship intact.

'One would be wise to cause no damage, milord,' Pierre suggested gently. 'True, as you say, before the Revolution it was permitted to the aristocrats to hunt as they pleased—'

'Then it must be now,' Sir Henry chimed in. 'You have your king back. All the decrees made by those revolutionary blackguards – and all Boney's new laws – they're washed out, abolished!'

'But these simple peasants are not yet used to the idea—'

'They'd better learn. Quick!'

Pierre shrugged. 'No doubt. But meanwhile, to avoid trouble – perhaps greater danger – it would be prudent, when riding over their land, to exercise some care.'

'Very well,' said Sir Henry sourly. Care, thought Ben, was the last thing he liked to exercise. Horses, hounds, himself, yes – but not care.

Ben would have liked more than one night in Rouen. The west front of the cathedral staggered him with its luxuriant Gothic decoration, so different from the classical simplicity of the London churches he knew best. What a back-drop, he thought, as it rose there, pale in the street lights, slashed with dramatic shadows! The houses too were a feast for the eye, stoutly timbered, with projecting gables and a wealth of carving, far older than almost any that survived in London.

The theatre was especially in his mind that evening. Sir Henry, anxious to make up for his neglect of Lady Mulroy during the day, took a box at the local playhouse. Pierre sat behind his employers, explaining the story in whispers. Ben bought a humbler place in the pit.

Unable to follow the plot, he found the play rather dull. He could sympathize with Lord Mulroy who, after a hard day in the saddle, seemed fast asleep whenever Ben looked up. Lady Mulroy and Sir Henry appeared to be happy enough. Ben himself could not fairly judge anything but the scenery, which struck him as shabby and unimaginative by Covent Garden standards. He would have like to give these foreigners a hint or two.

Not that they would have taken them. From the unfriendly stares of his neighbours he sensed that the English were not popular here. There were nudges and glances. Certain lines spoken by the actors produced inordinate applause. He began to suspect that the play contained a number of gibes against his country. When one comic character entered, an obvious caricature of an English squire, he was left in no doubt.

Nor was Sir Henry. As the scene continued, Ben could see him fidgeting. And when the curtain fell at the end of the act, there was a loud disturbance which turned every eye upon the box occupied by the tourists.

Sir Henry was bellowing and shaking his fist at a bearded Frenchman in the next box.

'You're laughing at *me*, sir? I'll make you laugh the other side of your face!'

Lady Mulroy was shrieking and preparing to swoon as Sir Henry coiled an arm round the intervening pillar and cocked one immense leg over the gilded balcony, as though to clamber across and assault the Frenchman.

'What the devil's the matter?' demanded Lord Mulroy, now fully awake.

'I'm going to pull Mounseer's beard!' announced Sir Henry.

The Frenchman was hurling back defiant insults. Pierre had slipped forward from the shadows and was trying, in two languages, to make the peace. The audience in general was finding it a better comedy even than the one being played on the stage. Foreseeing even worse trouble, Ben pushed his way out of the pit – cursed, hindered, once even tripped by the other occupants of the row – and ran up the staircase. He reached the door of Sir Henry's box just as it was flung open and Sir Henry came stamping out, to a background of whistles and cat-calls from the auditorium.

'I'll not sit there a minute longer and watch my country ridiculed!'

The Mulroys fluttered at his heels. 'Now I shall never know how the play ended!' her ladyship was protesting, to which her husband retorted, '*I* never knew how it began, my dear.'

The bearded gentleman had emerged from the adjoining box. Egged on by half a dozen friends, he seemed disposed to continue the quarrel.

'He requires an apology, milord,' Pierre interpreted with a worried expression.

'He requires a shave – and a bath, I don't doubt!' thundered Sir Henry. 'Tell him: all *I'm* prepared to give him is a sound thrashing, if he'll step outside.'

Ben could not tell how literally Pierre translated this reply, but he guessed that the courier was using great diplomacy. He took the opportunity to edge forward himself and take his stand at Sir Henry's elbow, casually flexing his muscles and adopting as ominous an expression as he could. The sight of another very tall Englishman seemed to have a calming effect upon their opponents. Whether it was due to that, or to Pierre's tact, or to the intercession of the distracted theatre-manager who appeared at that moment, the incident ended without bloodshed.

It seemed wise to quit Rouen next morning. 'Shall I lay out your hunting-coat?' Ben asked when calling Sir Henry.

'Yes. Well . . . perhaps no. I'm not sure. Yes, lay it out.'

Later, while the quality dallied over breakfast, Jupp came out with hopeless rolling eyes and reported to the servants the latest state of the game. 'Still nothing settled! Her ladyship's all for pressing on to Paris.'

'Eager for the gaieties of the capital,' said Doyle slyly.

'She's heard it's barely ninety miles. The public diligence does it in a day.'

'Then she's mad to be off, I'll be bound.'

'But his lordship isn't. Says the pack can't move at that rate.'

'I should think not!' The Irishman snorted with outrage. 'They should take a week for such a distance. And the horses too. If they're not to be ruined entirely.'

'You can imagine what your mistress says to a week in the barouche,' said Jupp grimly. 'She asked his lordship why the devil he could not leave the huntsman to bring on the infernal dogs at their own pace.'

'She called them that?' Doyle chuckled, scandalized. 'But she would.'

Ben could understand the complications. Moving the whole establishment across country was not easy. Not every posting inn could provide for such a party at short notice, and the fox-hounds presented a special problem. The huntsman and his assistants, without a word of French between them, would never manage. Even the resourceful courier could not be in two places at once – and if Lady Mulroy got her way, and pressed on to Paris at top speed, Pierre would certainly be needed to smooth the journey and find suitable accommodation at the other end.

Finally, black as thunder, Lady Mulroy took her solitary seat in the barouche. His lordship went off cheerfully with his pack, sounding a merry call on his horn which brought the people of Rouen to their windows. Sir Henry changed into his hunting-coat and mounted his second horse, Galliard. After a tart remark from Lady Mulroy, however, he did not ride off to overtake the others, but for the whole of that morning kept abreast of the barouche, talking to her through the window.

'I can't see how this tour is going to end,' said Jupp gloomily. 'Even a circus must travel with a plan.'

8 Unpleasantness at the Palais Royal

So, by fits and starts, the establishment continued its leisurely advance upon Paris.

Lord Mulroy hated cities and did not care if they never arrived. He seized every excuse to dally – a lame horse, a sick hound, or a missing falcon. It was seldom easy to find adequate accommodation, so, once the party was comfortably installed at an inn, it seemed reasonable to stay some days.

His lordship had an uncanny flair for nosing out the sporting facilities of each locality. If there was a fine stretch of river for angling, he heard of it. So too with partridges and pheasants. It was still early for fox-hunting, but not too late for stags. He had hopes of wolf and wild boar. He had never killed either and looked forward to the experience.

'We might as well have stayed at home amid our Irish bogs,' grumbled Lady Mulroy. Sir Henry was torn between them. He frankly enjoyed the sport, but he shared the gorgeous Georgina's yearning for a change of scene. Ben felt sorry for his master when she sulked and complained. Lady Mulroy should have learned to manage her husband.

Ben himself was quite happy with this unhurried pace. The other servants might grumble, despising foreigners, missing the beef and beer of home. He was entranced with the novelty of everything. His sketchbook was his shield against boredom. When the party lingered in a town, he had hours off duty to roam freely, sketching old abbeys, water-mills and markets, or trying to capture in a few deft strokes a grandmother in a doorway, making lace, or a woodman trudging along a forest ride.

True, his freedom was not always complete. Lady Mulroy would steal up behind, bending over his shoulder, powerfully perfumed, studying his work. She had forgiven him for that unflattering likeness of herself.

'Ben,' she would coo, 'I have found a ruined tower. Most romantic! It positively *breathes* Gothic fantasy.'

Then, hiding his resentment, he must break off and sketch it for her. Sir Henry's orders. He must do whatever she wished. Sometimes she merely required his attendance on a walk. A lady could scarcely go unattended, especially in a foreign land. The two gentlemen were so often at their sport. It must be Ben.

This unwanted favour did not endear him to the other servants. Unhappy at first in their hostility, he ended by shrugging his shoulders. All right. Come to that, *he* did not think much of *them*. He was not made for what they termed 'good service'. He did not want to turn into another Jupp, still less another Doyle. Nor did he want to be Lady Mulroy's spaniel, walking to heel.

So far, he seemed to have performed his duties to Sir

Henry's satisfaction. Packing and unpacking, brushing and boot-cleaning, were easy enough. He had picked up enough French phrases to cope with the inn people. He could find a laundress quickly, and ensure that Sir Henry's soiled linen would be back before breakfast, spotless and smoothed and starched where necessary. He learned how to obtain whatever Sir Henry shouted for, whether a purging draught at daybreak or a comforting cup of negus, hot, sweet and spicy, at bedtime. The work was mostly common sense and elbow-grease. But he did not intend to do it all his life.

It was with the French courier that he really made friends. Brought up to regard Napoleon's armies as a horde of monsters trampling Europe underfoot, he was fascinated by Pierre's quite different account of life in the hussars.

Pierre was thankful to have missed the appalling hardships of the retreat from Moscow two years before. 'It was terrible for the horses, too,' he said. 'And you understand, if one is hussar, one loves one's horse like oneself.'

Ben tactfully changed the subject. 'You have seen Italy,' he said enviously.

'Yes. Italy was the best. Afterwards, there was Spain.' Pierre smiled. 'I did not fear the English there. Do not misunderstand – you English fought hard, yes, and bravely, and we learned a great respect for your Wellington. But if the English beat us, they took prisoners. The Spanish guerrillas did not.' His face clouded. 'Or, if they did, it was better for a Frenchman to have fallen in the battle. I was fortunate. For me the war is finished in an English prison.'

'You must be glad it's all over now.'

'Of course. But now I must commence a new life.'

Pierre clearly meant to make the best of it. But he did not hide from Ben his admiration for Bonaparte or his contempt for Louis. 'The Emperor was not a tyrant,' he insisted, 'but the enemy of tyrants. And not only a great general – he made laws, he built roads, he wished to unite all Europe—'

'I think you'd like him back,' said Ben with a smile.

'But of course! So would every true Frenchman.'

'Don't let Sir Henry hear you.'

'No. One is prudent, naturally. I am courier now, not hussar.'

Even Lord Mulroy could not for ever postpone their arrival in Paris.

Now the autumn rains started. The roads grew muddier. 'All the more reason to stay where we are,' he argued. 'You sit by a good fire, my dear, while Harry and I go forth and brave the elements.'

'I did not cross the Channel to frowst by the fireside. I want Paris,' said Lady Mulroy implacably.

'But the pheasant season is beginning!'

'So is the season in Paris. There will be operas and balls and receptions. With the King back, and all the nobility, Paris will be so fashionable again.'

This time she had her way. Rebellious and protesting, his lordship allowed himself to be driven into the capital. Pierre, efficient as always, found kennels and stabling just outside. The main party was lucky to find accommodation at the Hotel d'Angleterre. 'It is said,' the courier explained, 'that there are twenty-five thousand British in Paris at this time.'

'It would be overcrowded even without them,' growled Jupp.

The servants, having grumbled every mile of the way from Le Havre, now complained no less of the city. They found the streets narrow and gloomy. The open gutters stank. There were no sidewalks to offer refuge from the traffic. If you hugged the wall you were apt to be drenched by the emptying of household buckets and worse from the upper windows, and if you walked in the middle you were trampled by horses or crushed by wheels.

But to Ben the wonders of Paris made up for all these dangers and inconveniences.

There was the vast palace of the Louvre, now turned into a museum and art gallery. Sir Henry, with his shrewd landowner's eye, vowed that it must cover forty acres. Ben was less interested in its acreage than in its contents.

If only old Linfoot were here to enjoy – and expound – this treasure-house of paintings and sculpture! Here was not just the art of France. In his conquests Napoleon had seized masterpieces everywhere, especially in Italy and Holland, despatching his loot to Paris by the waggon-load. Now it was all being sorted out so that it would be returned to its rightful owners. Until then, it was displayed along those echoing galleries, an exhibition such as had never been brought together under one roof before. Even Lady Mulroy thought it worth two visits, with Sir Henry's arm to lean on and Ben a respectful ten paces behind.

Ben himself returned again and again, when off duty. Sketching a marble Venus or a dying Gaul, he felt he had started to fulfil Linfoot's instructions. Yet much as he enjoyed his hours in the Louvre, sometimes inspired by those superb masterpieces, sometimes discouraged because he could never hope to rival them, the living Paris outside appealed to him even more.

There were, of course, the set spectacles, when King Louis went in state to attend Mass at Notre-Dame or reviewed a splendid parade of troops on the Champs de Mars. The corpulent, unmilitary monarch was quite overshadowed, thought Ben, by the Duke of Wellington riding with quiet dignity behind him. And there were gala nights at the Opéra and the Théâtre Français, where the scenic effects could have been improved upon, in Ben's opinion, but everything else was exceedingly fine.

Most, though, he loved the everyday life of the city, from those early hours when, Sir Henry still asleep, he could steal out to find the markets astir and the autumn mists wreathing up magically from the river, to the lamp-bright evenings when Lady Mulroy took a fancy to explore the boulevards. Pierre, as guide and interpreter, walked with her ladyship and Sir Henry. Ben played the faithful shadow, watchful for cutpurses or more violent characters. He was not 'with' the party in front and must never show any sign of recognition. If they entered a café, as the French termed their coffee-houses, he must watch discreetly from another table.

'I'm not afraid of any damned mounseer alive,' said Sir Henry, 'but I'll not have her ladyship annoyed. And I don't want to be thinking about my wallet the whole time.'

Even more than the boulevards Lady Mulroy delighted in the Palais Royal, where a long oblong garden was surrounded by arcades of luxurious shops and places of entertainment. 'One can buy anything here,' said Pierre, adding under his breath, 'and almost any one.' She could have her hair done in the latest style at Sainte-Foix's, while a few doors away at Colman's Sir Henry could be fitted for a pair of seamless boots. There were twenty-four jewellers alone and countless dealers in silks and laces and exquisite porcelain. Sir Henry could never bear her to leave the Palais Royal without some keepsake that had taken her fancy. Or possibly, thought Ben, it would be truer to say that he could not bear her sulks if she did.

Each expedition followed a pattern. Lord Mulroy was soon bored by the shops. Ben would watch amusedly as his lord-ship's bow legs took him gradually further and further ahead, until he was lost completely in the crowd. One thing was predictable: by the time his wife had fallen in love with some article, and the shopkeeper was purring over an assured sale, Lord Mulroy would be far away and Sir Henry would be fumbling for his money.

Seventeen billiard-saloons opened off the arcades, and almost as many gaming-houses. Lord Mulroy would be seen no more that night. It would have taken hours to run him to earth, and Lady Mulroy was not one to waste her time in that way. Were there not fifteen different restaurants serving de-licious suppers in the Palais Royal, and almost twice that number of cafés offering light refreshments?

'Humphy will find his way back,' she would assure Sir Henry. 'He always does.'

And Sir Henry would smile down at her gallantly and murmur his usual answer, 'Whatever you say, my dear.'

The freedom of Paris was much to Lady Mulroy's taste. Here a woman of rank could 'play the vagabond', as she termed it – which meant that, so long as she had a gentleman as escort, she would eat and drink in public places and go more or less wherever she chose, in a manner that would have caused much raising of old-fashioned eyebrows at home.

Of all the cafés in the Palais Royal she was particularly fond of the Mille Colonnes. This was run by an impressive beauty, splendid in crimson velvet and flashing with diamonds, said to have once enjoyed the love of the exiled Emperor. She presided at a raised table with a golden inkstand. She had such presence, one might have said she was enthroned. The waiters scurried tirelessly under her keen supervision, and everything was excellent.

Ben never forgot his first visit. Having found an obscure corner for himself, he asked for a glass of punch. To his embarrassment he was brought a fair-sized bowl of the delicious liquor, heavily iced. It seemed a pity to waste it, especially when he learned the price, though Sir Henry was generous enough in allowing for such expenditure. Ben finished the bowl, and with great enjoyment, feeling unusually light-hearted and uncertain of balance for the rest of that evening. Fortunately nothing cropped up to test his sobriety.

Pierre laughed when Ben told him. 'But of course! You asked for a 'glass' in English? To the waiter "*glace*" would mean only "ice".'

Ben decided to be more diligent in his study of the French language, before his mistakes became more serious.

Their final visit to the Café des Mille Colonnes was just as memorable, but for a quite different reason.

That evening the place was crowded and it was hard to find tables. Pierre was not there to help. His presence was no longer required on every expedition, and in the Palais Royal his employer now felt completely at home.

Sir Henry shouldered his way in, and, by looming over a small table, and scowling down at an innocent young couple who had just finished their coffee, intimidated them into hasty departure. Ben, at the same moment, was lucky to find a vacant place at the next table. Ordinarily, he would have sat further away, keeping his party under observation without overhearing their talk. That night he had no choice.

He was immediately aware of a change in Sir Henry's manner to her ladyship. Could it be that the worm at last had turned? The pair were actually in dispute.

Lady Mulroy said, petulantly: 'I imagined you would be pleased. It's a piece of luck – this château, vacant, ready for occupation, so close to Paris, sporting facilities of every sort to keep poor Humphy amused. Indeed it offers the best of both worlds. Surely the *rent* does not deter you? To any one of your means, the expense is nothing—'

'Confound the expense! Though it is not *nothing*. You can scarcely complain that I am mean, Georgina—'

'I wonder. Sometimes you calculate—'

'Hang it, I *must* calculate!'

'A person of the finest breeding is above such sordid considerations.'

'Will *you* forget money for a moment, then?' Sir Henry's glare could have cracked the wine-glasses. 'You said yourself, we came over to see the Continent. It has taken us all these weeks – fighting Humphrey every yard of the way – to get as far as Paris. Now you want to settle here for the rest of the winter – move into some dam' great draughty château on the outskirts – so that you can drive in and out to enjoy yourself in town and Humph shan't miss a day's hunting. Hang it, I might as well have rented a place in Surrey.'

'Then what would you prefer to do?' Her tone was icy.

'Move on,' he said without hesitation.

'At this time of year? My dear Harry, the roads – the weather—'

'Not too bad if we make for the south. You used to talk of Venice. And Naples. Gad! Travelling at this pace, we'll be a hundred before we see Italy.'

Ben no longer tried to avoid eavesdropping. While staring tactfully in every other direction, he kept his ears cocked.

'I still *want* to see Italy.' Lady Mulroy was plaintive now.

'Then let's go!'

'How can we? Without Humphy? I must think of my reputation.'

'You should get him away from Paris. He's losing too much at cards.'

'I *know*, Harry! But he'll only budge for one thing. He likes the idea of this château—'

'I like sport as much as the next man. But, devil take it, Georgina, Humph is obsessed!'

'He's my husband, remember! Of course, we shall have to do what *you* want in the end. We *are* your guests.'

'Oh, confound that!' Furious, Sir Henry signalled for the waiter. 'Time I took you back. You must think of your reputation!' He paid the reckoning, tossing the gold louis violently upon the table. Then he almost bundled her ladyship out into the night, and Ben had to move smartly to pay for his own drink and follow them.

It was tantalizing to miss the rest of the argument, but in the street he had to keep his distance. However, he was not left long in doubt as to the result. Sir Henry leapt from his bed next morning with the glee of a schoolboy at the start of the holidays.

'Ah! Morning, Ben! A clean shave, this morning! We'll be on parade. Straight after breakfast. A call upon the Duke of Wellington.'

'*Wellington*, sir?'

'He's the British ambassador in Paris, ain't he? We'll need new passports. We're off to Italy.'

Ben almost dropped the steaming water. Sir Henry snatched his razor with alarming exuberance. As he scraped, he unfolded his plans. He was renting an estate in the forest outside Paris. It would take a day or two to settle things with the confounded lawyers. Once the papers were signed, he would leave that old rascal Jupp to get on with it. Jupp could move the whole establishment into this château. Lord and Lady Mulroy would go with them. 'Hang it, they *are* my guests. Least I can do. But I told them straight last night, *I* came abroad to see Europe.'

'So you gave me to understand, sir, when you engaged me.'

'And I'm a man of my word. You and I will go to Italy.'

Ben stood transfixed, dropping lather on the floor. 'You

mean, sir – *alone*?' The idea was both attractive and disturbing. 'Without even Pierre?'

'Jupp will need Pierre, to handle the natives. Pierre will go to the château with the others.' Sir Henry turned his great head and fixed Ben with a challenging scowl. 'Don't you feel competent to look after me on your own?'

Not for the world would Ben have admitted that. But he felt compelled to say modestly, 'I have no training as a valet, sir—'

'Valet be hanged! You won't be a valet,' his master assured him with more cheerfulness than Ben himself felt. 'You'll have to do everything. You'll be – what's the word? – a factotum.'

So it was decided. But in the whirl of impetuous preparations that followed, Ben sometimes wondered whether the word should not really have been teetotum.

9 To see the monster

Until the last moment Ben expected Sir Henry to change his mind. Surely Lady Mulroy's tears – or tongue – would dissuade him? The quarrel would blow over. Sir Henry's devotion would become even more abject than before.

Seemingly not. That gentleman's simmering resentment had boiled over, and the mood was lasting. The essential arrangements were completed with surprising speed.

Lady Mulroy stood on her dignity, Sir Henry on his. Ben secretly hugged himself.

His master, having said so much about travelling, was now committed to going. Downstairs with his friends, where the atmosphere was strained, he was compelled for form's sake to talk big about the sights he longed to see.

In the privacy of his own room, however, he betrayed some

vagueness. All at once, with the loss of Lady Mulroy's enchanting companionship, the far-off places had waned in their appeal. Was it really worth going to Venice? Or Rome? Rome was called 'the eternal city', so presumably it would still be there in six months' time, when he might hope to explore it with Lady Mulroy on his arm. Ruins that had stood for so many centuries could surely be trusted to stand until next year? As for Naples, Florence and Genoa, Sir Henry considered each in turn, and Ben's heart sank when he realized how much of the original enthusiasm had evaporated.

It was Elba that saved the situation.

Pierre, usually so discreet, let slip a remark suggesting that his late emperor was not the monster imagined by the English.

Sir Henry's face darkened. 'Poppycock!' It was plainly reported in all the newspapers, wasn't it? Bonaparte, now that he had time to reflect upon his crimes against humanity, was haunted by guilt. 'Can't sleep at night,' said Sir Henry. 'He dreams of blood.' Triumphantly he quoted various paragraphs from the press. The deposed despot had gone mad. Marooned on this tiny Italian islet which had become his kingdom, he was behaving as though he were still master of Europe.

'He has a navy! Four tiny vessels – it says here, the *Caroline* carries only a single gun!' Sir Henry laughed until the veins swelled on his temples. 'We've let him keep a few veterans of the Guard and some Polish lancers. No horses, though! Only allowed their saddles. Lancers without horses! Still, they can put their saddles on hobby-horses, I suppose – or clothes-horses.' He spluttered and almost choked. 'Boney's formed them into an army. Marches them across his little island – and then marches them back again! Been playing at soldiers all his life. Can't stop.'

Ben felt sorry for the courier, listening tight-lipped. Pierre said politely: 'All this is in our French newspapers, milord. And even wilder stories, scandals that cannot possibly be true. One should not believe every word from the journalists.'

'Ha! Think they're fooling us, do you?' Sir Henry grew

belligerent. 'Let me tell you this, then. I'm going to Elba. See for myself. It'll give me the greatest pleasure to see this emperor of yours – like a wild beast in a menagerie!'

This idea fired him with fresh determination. Ben was vastly relieved. He himself had no wish to gloat over the beaten enemy, but they could scarcely reach Elba without seeing a good deal of Italy on the way.

They had to attend upon the Duke of Wellington again with their passports. His Grace – with rather icy disapproval, Ben fancied – endorsed the documents to permit their landing on the island. It was Ben's task to make the travelling arrangements. Sir Henry went to his Paris banker and then gave Ben ample cash to cover the first stage of their journey.

'We'll go free as the air, just the two of us,' he announced, with a paralysing slap between Ben's shoulder-blades. 'We'll use the public diligence. Less fuss.' His own carriage would go to the château with the establishment.

Pierre was helpful over the best route to follow, the scale of tips, and the art of dealing with drivers and conductors. Ben duly found his way to the coaching office in the Rue Montmartre and secured two places for the following afternoon as far as Troyes. The clerk scribbled '38' on a scrap of paper, which was clearly the fares. Ben put down two golden napoleons – everyone still seemed to call them that, though officially they had changed their name to *louis d'or*. Anyhow, they were still worth twenty francs each. He picked up his two francs change and entered the item in his account-book. He meant to record every detail of expenditure. With Sir Henry it was best to take no chances.

The last twenty-four hours were full of suspense.

Relations between his master and the Mulroys continued civil but chilly. At any moment, up to the last, they might completely change. He overheard Sir Henry assuring his guests that Jupp would look after them.

'Treat the place as your own till I join you. Only sorry you won't come to Elba with me. Hope you'll find the sport good, Humphrey. Take care of yourselves.'

'And I hope *you* will take good care of yourself,' said her ladyship, looking daggers. 'I hear that the Italian bandits are quite remorseless.'

'You needn't be concerned, Georgina. There's not a bandit living will lay a finger on *us*.' Sir Henry slapped his chest, which at least (thought Ben with feeling) was a welcome variant from slapping other people on the back.

The other servants made no pretence of sorrow at the loss of Ben's company. He was still an outsider and they were glad to see him go. They were looking forward to a lazy time until their difficult master returned. When Ben had Horsewhip Harry to himself, he would discover what he was really like.

'If you don't stand up to him, he'll walk right over you,' said Doyle. 'And if you do stand up to him, he'll knock you down. You'll never stay the course.'

'We'll see,' said Ben.

Only Pierre showed real regret. He escorted them to the Rue Montmartre at three o'clock the next afternoon and helped Ben to check the bags with the conductor. This man, seeing the size of his two English passengers, wanted Ben to ride on the top of the coach. Ben might have agreed, but Pierre would not let him.

'You will be frozen! It is December – and you will be travelling all night. This rascal is only trying to get your seat for someone else.' He demolished the conductor with a burst of French, which Ben partly understood. He gathered that 'the English milords' (it was amusing to be thus promoted to the nobility) had paid for two seats inside the diligence, and two seats they must have.

And they did, wedged side by side, so that Sir Henry's girth caused no inconvenience to anyone but Ben, who twisted and squeezed himself into the corner as best he could.

What did it matter? They were off! The yellow lights of Paris bobbed and blurred behind them. They were clattering through the twilit countryside. Neither the smiles nor the tears of Lady Mulroy could overtake them now.

He was thankful, though, as the endless winter's night wore on, that Pierre had insisted on the inside place. Even the thick greatcoat Sir Henry had equipped him with could not keep out the invading cold. And, though there was straw underfoot, his toes felt frozen inside his boots.

Brief halts at stages offered a chance to stretch legs, swing arms and stamp feet on the cobbles, while fresh horses were harnessed. But not until ten o'clock next morning was there a real stop, to take breakfast. Never had crisp warm bread and scalding coffee tasted so good. Sir Henry, however, glowered at the coarse earthenware cups with their clumsy handles.

'Not going to drink out of *this*! Ask 'em for a decent china cup. Tell 'em this is the sort of article we'd keep under the bed in England.'

Ben did not transmit this complaint in full. He managed to obtain a more seemly vessel for his master's coffee, though it cost him precious minutes of his own breakfast-time. The diligence waited little more than a quarter of an hour. He hoped Sir Henry would not always be making such difficulties.

They had to wait for dinner until they reached Troyes. By then it was dark again. Sir Henry's good humour returned when he saw a substantial meal before him. 'Champagne!' he ordered. 'Made in these parts, ain't it?'

'Most appropriate, sir.' It was always best to agree with Sir Henry, and, as Ben saw the pale wine frothing and sparkling into their glasses, he had no wish to do otherwise on this occasion.

Their new mode of travel was very different. Now he was with his master the whole day, and it seemed likely that he was to be with him all night as well. The inn had big rooms upstairs with several beds, each in a curtained recess. Complete strangers shared these rooms. Sir Henry might curse and complain, but there was no alternative. Finally, being tired, and mellow with champagne, he accepted the situation.

They saw all they wanted to see of Troyes the next morning. Sir Henry was keen to press on, and Ben did not discourage him. He managed to book places on the Dijon coach, leaving at six that evening. It meant another night journey, cold and cramped. When daylight came at last, he was not in the best mood to appreciate the scenery, though it was getting wilder and more picturesque. A long day followed. It was half-past six in the evening when they rumbled into the ancient capital of Burgundy. Pierre had recommended an hotel much patronized by the English gentry, and soon they were sitting down to another excellent meal.

Ben chose his moment when Sir Henry had called for a second bottle of red wine. 'I'm afraid we must stay here two nights, sir. It seems that the Geneva coach starts at five in the morning. I thought that a little excessive – after today.'

'All right. This place will do me well enough.'

After a late breakfast they took a turn round the ramparts in the pale wintry sunshine. There were fine views, finer still when they climbed the cathedral tower. Far in the distance snow-capped peaks gleamed above a swathe of cloud. With a quickening of the pulse, not solely due to the steps they had mounted, Ben knew that one dream had been realized: he was gazing at the Alps. That was the way they would go tomorrow. Everything was working out splendidly.

They would need to rise at four. He packed that evening, keeping out only their night-things, and sent the bags round to the coach-office. He settled the bill. No time for disputes in the morning. He was getting the hang of his duties.

This was the longest stretch of their journey so far, about a hundred and twenty miles. After an early halt for dinner at Dole they changed into a curious vehicle which took only three passengers, sitting sideways. The conductor assured them that it was the best kind of carriage for the mountains in December.

'Deucedly uncomfortable,' grumbled Sir Henry. 'Bad as those jaunting cars at Lord Muroy's place in Ireland. Except that it's covered, thank Heaven.'

He was, however, in a good humour. He could hardly wait to cross the frontier and quit the country of the sly mounseers. He was irritable only when they had to pull in to allow a regiment to march by. What right had the French to keep an army, after being so soundly beaten? His indignation grew when they saw, bringing up the rear, what looked like half a dozen boys on horseback. These proved on closer observation to be officers' wives in men's clothing.

'Disgusting! But what can you expect of the immoral French?'

Ben privately found them attractive. Backstage, it was common enough to see actresses dressed for 'breeches parts' like Rosalind or Jessica. He was not shocked. He thought wistfully of Sal.

Darkness fell. They began to climb into the Jura mountains and their pace slackened. The road narrowed and grew rough. At times he felt, rather than saw, that they were creeping along the lip of some horrific precipice. The carriage-lamps glimmered on tufted treetops, rising from roots unbelievably far down the slope. The odd sideways seating gave a vivid sense of the dizzy abyss below the windows.

The winter sunrise made the endless night worthwhile. The snowfields sparkled pink as roses. He saw, with a thrill of discovery, that the long shadows of the pines were not grey but blue.

They were driving through the mountains all day. Only as the red sun dropped behind the black edge of the west did the road begin its long descent towards Geneva. Even Sir Henry was a little subdued when they walked stiffly into the Hotel de l'Ecu after seven o'clock that evening.

Next morning, however, they woke to a scene which again, for Ben at least, made up for the weariness of the previous day.

Lake Léman spread below the window. Dramatic mountains hung like tapestry. Shimmering scarves of mist trailed across them, so that the cut-off summits appeared to float like islands in the sky.

Ben longed to get to work with his watercolours, but it was with Sir Henry's shaving water that he had to concern himself, Sir Henry's breakfast fads, the state of Sir Henry's inside, and the clean linen to cover Sir Henry's substantial exterior.

Surely though, after the rigours of a week's travel, his master would be content to linger in this beautiful place. Why travel at all, if you never stayed long enough to see anything?

Sir Henry was of a different mind. The desire to see Napoleon had become an obsession. His dislike of the French, devoloped through years of war, had been sharpened by meeting them in their own country and discovering that they were not ashamed of themselves. In Paris there had been rumours of an unsuccessful plot, involving hundreds of the Emperor's former officers. At Troyes and Dijon it had been evident that there was still a great deal of Bonapartist feeling. Sir Henry could not wait to reach Elba and feast his eyes on the spectacle of the captive conqueror.

There was another reason for haste. 'There's talk in the newspapers of shifting him,' he told Ben. 'The Allied governments think Elba's too near, and the old fox might escape. He'd be safer in the West Indies. There's even talk of putting him on some godforsaken rock in the middle of the Atlantic, St Helena or somewhere. And so they should! But I mean to see him before he goes.'

'Surely, sir, that's unlikely to happen yet? It'll take time for all the governments to agree.'

'I tell you, Ben, I'm going to land on Elba, and have a good look at old Boney, before the year is out.'

Ben's face fell. 'I doubt if we can manage *that*, sir. A few days can make no difference.'

But Sir Henry now had the bit between his teeth.

'No,' he insisted, 'even the first of January, 1815, *ain't* the same as the thirty-first of December, 1814, and don't you try to persuade me it is! This year, I said, and this year I meant. You get down to that coaching-office and do what you're paid for.' He scowled at Ben with less than his usual friendliness.

Ben saw the danger signal and said no more.

So, tantalizingly, they pursued their way past glistening lakes and foaming waterfalls, through romantic pine-forests and along the edges of awful chasms. Ben's sketchbook was seldom unpacked. The jolting of the coach made it impossible to set down even the crudest impressions of the grandeur through which they were being carried, mile after mile. When they halted, either it was dark or his fingers were too numb to hold a pencil or Sir Henry was demanding some immediate attention. Ben could only strive desperately to store his mind with visual images, which one day with luck he might incorporate in a picture. Or perhaps, if he were given the chance, in a drop-scene for some opera or melodrama at Covent Garden. What transparencies one could design, when the whole sky changed colour behind the silhouetted Alps and the lights began winking from the windows of these picturesque log houses!

They crossed the Simplon Pass by a superb road which (Sir Henry was furious to learn, too late, after he had praised it) was the work of Napoleon's military engineers. Good as the road was, it took them from seven in the morning until four o'clock the next day to get across it. The winter snows had started. Their coach had to be taken off its wheels and placed on sledge-runners. Last year, said the conductor, the diligence had fallen down the slope and buried itself in the drifts far below.

And now – as the voices, the faces, the sunshine, the very names on the signposts told them: Domodossola, what music in the syllables! – they were in Italy. Ben's heart leapt. Italy! The painter's promised land.

Still Sir Henry's impatience would allow no dallying. Down the widening valleys, past the sapphire expanse of Lake Maggiore, on, on, to Milan, Pavia, Genoa, and their first sight of the Mediterranean.

When they were not actually on the move, Ben's waking hours seemed to be a never-ending war with coaching-offices, innkeepers, policemen and others. All the frontiers altered by Napoleon were being altered back again, and until the peace was finally settled at Vienna none of the different Italian regions knew quite where it belonged. The money was a muddle. The lira was much the same as a French franc, but at Genoa it turned out to be a Sardinian lira and worth less. At posthouses he was asked to pay in Spanish dollars. Often, if he did not look out, he was given Roman scudi or Neapolitan carolines in his change. Somehow he had to keep his accounts in order. Like many rich men, Sir Henry could suddenly turn strict, almost miserly.

Language was another difficulty. The French he had picked up was only of limited use among the Italians. Sir Henry discovered that when, in his perverse fashion, he rummaged in his mind for the French he had once had flogged into him as a boy. It seemed to him unreasonable that Italians should not at least understand French. They were all foreigners, weren't they? Well then!

To cap everything, the weather turned against them. As they followed the coast down to Spezia, the sun vanished and sodden rain-clouds came drifting in from the sea.

'But, hang it,' Sir Henry complained, 'this isn't what I expected of the *Mediterranean*!' He seemed aggrieved that he could not reject it, like some disappointing dish sent back to the kitchen. One miserable evening, as they huddled over a tiny stove in a flea-ridden hostelry at Chiavari, Ben realized from the date in his account-book that it was Christmas Eve.

It made no difference. They pushed on, delayed only by a broken coach-wheel one day and a landslide, due to the rain, that blocked the road another. They hurried through Pisa, Sir Henry sparing a few minutes to gape at the Leaning Tower. At Leghorn they found that, because of the storms, no vessel was sailing to Elba. They could either wait indefinitely, or hire a post-chaise and drive further south to Piombino. By then, the weather might have picked up. And from there, as the map plainly showed, it was a very short crossing to the island.

'We'll hire,' said Sir Henry. 'Can't bear to hang about doing nothing.'

Nothing was ever simple. Ben had to inquire, as best he could, and then haggle. The Italians would do nothing without bargaining. If you gave way at once, he discovered, they were so disappointed at missing their usual amusement that they changed their minds and went back on their original offer, so that the negotiation had to begin all over again. In his blacker moments he began to agree with Sir Henry that they were beset by rogues on every side.

It was, he saw, December the thirtieth . . .

With the finding of a post-chaise and driver, their luck changed. The rain stopped. Despite deep ruts and potholes, they accomplished the day's drive to Piombino without mis-adventure. Towards sunset the wind dropped and the sky cleared. As they entered the town they saw across the six-mile strait of golden water, silhouetted as in the Covent Garden transparency, the rugged island to which the Emperor had been banished.

The calm weather held overnight. After breakfast next day, the last day of 1814, a highly satisfied Sir Henry marched down the gangway of the local ferry-boat and landed on Elba.

10 A girl in a violet dress

They found quarters in what looked like the only possible inn. Portoferraio was a dreary little town of flaking yellow houses. Narrow lanes, steep as staircases, ran up from the waterfront.

'At least, sir,' said Ben cheerfully, indicating the names in the register, 'some English people have stayed here before. Several dozen, in fact, in the last few months.'

After dinner they went to pay a courtesy call upon the British Commissioner.

Sir Neil Campbell welcomed them warmly. He struck Ben as a very intelligent man, full of common sense and toleration. His only obvious handicap was a slight deafness, but for anyone listening to Sir Henry this could be almost an advantage.

'See the Emperor?' he said. 'Nothing easier. He's out and about a good deal. Not so much lately, perhaps – must be the winter weather. But in the summer he used to be up at five, digging and ploughing and going out with the fishing-boats.

He'd ride for hours in the afternoons. At present he more often uses his carriage. Anyhow, you'll have plenty of chances to see him. Talk to him, if you like.'

'Really?' Sir Henry's eyes gleamed.

'Why not? He has talked to various British tourists. It's confoundedly dull for us all here – and worse for him.'

'You sound sympathetic!' said Sir Henry accusingly.

'Perhaps I am. He's human, like the rest of us.'

'I wonder! I thought it was your duty as British Commissioner to keep an eye on the fellow.'

'So I do. But, my dear sir, I'm not a *jailer*. And he is not a prisoner. He rules here. His formal title is "Emperor, and Sovereign of the Isle of Elba".'

'He's just Bonaparte to me. A jumped-up general.'

'Then I must ask you to conceal your opinion, if I present you to him.' Sir Neil's tone had stiffened. 'The Emperor will be deeply insulted if you address him as "General Bonaparte".'

'I shall give him the respect he deserves, no more, no less. We won the war, didn't we? He's only an exile here! Yet you let him put on all these airs!'

'I follow my instructions, Sir Henry. And I think that the best way to "keep an eye on the fellow" – as you term it – is to remain on cordial terms with him. We have had some very interesting conversations. We get on very well.'

'I am sure you do,' said Sir Henry with heavy sarcasm. 'What I'm less sure of is this: can you guarantee he won't make a bolt for it if he wants to? Can you stop him?'

Sir Neil shrugged. 'I have no armed force at my disposal – ashore, that is. You may have seen the brig anchored in the harbour?'

'The *Partridge*, sir?' Ben ventured to put in a word. Sir Henry had introduced him as his 'young companion'. The status of 'valet' had been quietly dropped, though in private Sir Henry still expected all the old obedience.

'Yes, Mr Reeth. Commander, Captain Adye. Officially, I have the *Partridge* at my disposal for crossings to the main-

mainland, visits to Leghorn, and so forth. In practice, the *Partridge* is available to make sure the Emperor does not leave the island.

'But, hang it!' cried Sir Henry. 'The fellow has his own ships – a toy navy—'

The Commissioner smiled. 'I think the brig is a match for them. Captain Adye has his orders. He is to intercept. And if he meets with the slightest resistance, he is to destroy. I do not think you need lose any sleep, Sir Henry. Behind the *Partridge* lies the whole might of the British Navy. In any case, I've no reason to suppose that the Emperor is considering any such folly.'

'You can't be sure!'

'I agree, I can't be sure. But he is watched on every side. The island is full of spies. French spies particularly—'

'French!' Sir Henry snorted.

'Of course,' said Sir Neil patiently. 'The French government – the new one, King Louis and our turncoat friend Talleyrand – *they're* the ones most frightened of his escaping. Their spies come over by almost every boat.' He chuckled. 'They dress up as friars and seamen and traders and heaven knows what else. They're so numerous, they can't know each other, so sometimes they spy on each other by mistake. They seize on the wildest rumours, and send them back to Paris, and then all manner of nonsense gets printed in the papers.'

Ben did not dare to look at Sir Henry. He could almost feel, physically, the glow of his master's indignation.

Sir Henry stood up and seized his hat. 'We cannot afford to be complacent, Sir Neil. I will take up no more of your valuable time.'

'Honoured, sir. Pleasant to see English faces.'

'You will send us word when you have arranged a meeting with Boney?'

'Of course.' Ben fancied that the Commissioner hesitated.

'It will give me immense pleasure,' said Sir Henry, 'to give the fellow a piece of my mind.'

'You speak French? Or perhaps Italian?'

'Devil a word!'

Sir Neil seized on this answer with obvious relief. 'Then it might be difficult. The Emperor does not speak English.'

'It's time he learned, I should think.'

'Perhaps, Sir Henry. Perhaps.' Sir Neil saw them out with perfect courtesy. 'Well – if anything can be managed, you will hear from me at your hotel.'

They walked away. 'Don't believe a word of it,' said Sir Henry, not troubling to keep his voice down. 'He doesn't mean us to get within a mile of Boney.' Ben had already formed that impression, and thought the Commissioner very sensible, but it would have been unwise to say so. 'He's smug. And weak. Not up to the job. May have been bribed, even.'

Ben was so shocked, he protested instinctively. 'Oh, you can't say that, sir—'

'Can't? And who the devil are you, to tell me what I can't say and what I can?'

'I meant no disrespect, sir, but—'

'But what?'

'Sir Neil is a gentleman, a man or honour—'

'That's *your* opinion,' said Sir Henry sourly.

'Yes, sir. And I have often heard you say, the glory of the British nation is every man's right to express an opinion of his own.'

'So it is! Don't try to bandy words with me, boy!'

What could one do with such a man? Ben remembered the Irish valet's ominous forecast. How much longer would he be able to stay the course?

The sun was setting. The tunny-fishing boats moored along the quays lifted bold black silhouettes against the fiery gold. Sir Henry wanted at least to see where Napoleon lived, so they walked on as far as the fortifications commanding the bay. Here, between two forts, Stella and Falcone, they found the Villetta dei Mulini, a not very impressive building to which, as they could see from the ladders and scaffolding, an extra storey was being added. A flag was just being hauled down by a soldier. Two more soldiers stood guard outside.

'Not much of a place,' said Sir Henry with obvious satisfaction. 'Bit of a come-down for old Boney! After lording it at Fontainebleau and the Tuileries! I'd like a picture of this. You can come back in the morning and draw me one.'

'Very good, sir.'

They turned back towards their inn. A clatter of hoofs signalled the approach of a carriage. Its lamps bobbed in the fading light. A few children came scuttling with excited cries. Some fishermen stood up, pulling off their caps.

'I think it's *him*, sir,' Ben murmured. Sir Henry stopped.

The carriage drew level. Ben caught a brief but unforgettable glimpse of a smallish man in a green tunic and white breeches – a pale-faced man, who for an instant turned and fixed them with a searching glance. Was it their height, in this land of shorter men – or was it that Sir Henry pointedly refrained from removing his hat?

The carriage went spanking by. It wheeled into the gateway of the Mulini, and they heard the clash of sentinels presenting arms. 'Put your hat on!' snarled Sir Henry. 'Or are you a confounded Bonapartist yourself?'

'Certainly not, sir. But it seemed only good manners—'

'Manners be hanged! No Englishman should bare his head to that scoundrel. Upon my soul, I sometimes wonder if your views are quite *sound*.'

Ben managed to avoid further argument. That evening, luckily, there was a performance in the new theatre which the Emperor had just converted for his subjects from a disused church. It was not an outstanding entertainment, a mixed bill of French comedy and Italian vaudeville, with an enthusiastic orchestra of twenty recruited from his bodyguard. At least it passed the rest of the day, and kept Sir Henry amused.

The morrow dawned fine, the air balmy, the Mediterranean all it was supposed to be. Ben felt that he already had his orders. So, without giving his master time to change his mind, he took his sketchbook and slipped away. There was a clean new bench commanding a view of the imperial residence from just the right angle. There were, indeed, new benches and lamps at intervals all along the waterfront. Somebody, presumably Elba's energetic sovereign, was clearly taking this shabby little town in hand. Ben sat down on the bench and got to work.

He was not left alone for long.

After about ten minutes an officer emerged from the building, smart in sky-blue uniform with silver piping. He greeted Ben civilly in French and peered over his shoulder. Ben braced himself for an argument, but none developed. 'Monsieur is an artist?' Ben would not have claimed the title for himself, but it was better to accept it. 'Very fine,' said the officer, much too flatteringly. Satisfied apparently that Ben was not another spy, he departed.

Far more disturbing were the ragged urchins. In the course of another quarter of an hour Ben had attracted about twenty of them. Only one or two tried to beg, and they gave up when no coin was forthcoming – he had been in Italy long enough to know it would be fatal to put his hand in his pocket. It was rather that they were fascinated by what he was doing. They crowded round, they bent over him, they thrust excited and grubby fingers perilously close to the white paper, they fought each other for vacant space on the bench so that they could squeeze close to this fascinating foreigner.

They jogged his arm. Their vibrant voices resounded like the chatter of an aviary, plying him with incomprehensible questions and exchanging vehement comments between themselves. Their unwashed bodies conquered even the harbour-smells and the light breeze from the open bay.

Somehow he must finish at least one sketch of the Mulini and the fort in the background. He could not face Sir Henry empty-handed. But his irritation and despair were growing – he had torn out and discarded one spoilt effort – when a fresh voice, a woman's, cut through the hubbub. What she said, he could not tell, since it was in Italian, but the ring of authority was unmistakable. Suddenly there was quiet. He had empty air at both elbows, the bench was abandoned. And from over his shoulder he was conscious of a very different perfume, a delicate fragrance that did not cling to the boys of Elba.

'*Scusi, signore.*' The voice was low, almost shy and apologetic, very different from the sound that had sent the urchins scuttling in retreat along the waterfront.

Politeness made him get up and turn to face her. He fumbled for the few Italian words he had so far learned. '*Grazie tanto, signora.*' And as he faced her, a slim dark girl in a violet dress, he wondered if he ought not to have called her '*signorina*'. She was no older than himself, but her gloves made it impossible to see whether she wore a ring. He wanted to thank her properly for getting rid of the boys, but did not know how to say it. '*Ingles,*' he explained.

'English?' she exclaimed.

'As English as you,' he said delightedly.

Her face showed no answering pleasure. 'I am not,' she said emphatically. 'Do I *sound* English?'

He realized now that she did not, and there was something in her speech that was neither Scots nor Irish. He asked hesitantly, 'Are you American?'

'I certainly am! And mighty sorry to have intruded upon you.'

He misunderstood her. 'You sent those boys running – they were the real distraction. I'm very grateful. If you wanted to look at my sketch – I've only just started again—' He held out his work shyly.

She backed away. 'Thank you,' she said coldly. 'I have no wish to talk to you.'

Her tone was like a slap in the face.

He stared at her in utter amazement. 'Have I offended you? What have I done?'

'It's what your countrymen have done. Or have you been too busy drawing pictures to notice? Britain is at war with the United States.'

He could have kicked himself. Of course! It had been going on for eighteen months. But in London it had seemed remote and unimportant. When your country was locked in a life-and-death struggle with France, just across the Channel, you did not spare much thought for what was happening in the New World three thousand miles away. And even less when you were touring Italy, and had not seen an English news-paper for more than a month.

He forced a smile. 'Does that mean that *we* have to fight? We're civilians – we meet on neutral territory—'

'There is no occasion for us to meet at all.' She faced him, standing very erect, bright-eyed, hot-cheeked. 'I made a fool-ish mistake, approaching you. I am interested in art, and—'

'Surely,' he pleaded, 'they say art should have nothing to do—'

But she cut him short. 'I know that I should have nothing to do with an Englishman. Your troops took Washington. They behaved like vandals. They burnt the White House – and the Capitol—'

He scarcely knew what she was talking about, but he could not mistake her anger. He groped for words. 'I'm sorry. I – I wish—'

'And *I* wish *you* – good-day.'

She turned on her heel and set off briskly towards the centre of the town, a slender determined figure in a violet dress that strained and rippled in the light breeze. It seemed to be the fashionable colour on the Continent this winter. Even some of the men, like Pierre, used ribbons of that hue instead of watch-chains. From Paris onwards he had noticed numerous ladies in violet. But not one he would remember as vividly as this young American.

As he watched, he saw the Emperor's carriage returning from an early drive. The girl not only paused at the roadside, but, as the carriage reached her, she actually bobbed a curtsy. And then, to Ben's mingled amusement and vexation, the car-riage pulled up, and he saw the girl run to it. For a full five minutes she stood there, her bonnet tilted upwards as she talked to some one leaning out of it. Then the carriage drove on again, and the girl looked after it, handkerchief fluttering. As it wheeled through the gates Ben saw that the solitary occupant was indeed Napoleon.

Well, what could you expect? The Emperor, it was common gossip, could never resist a pretty woman. And to the American girl, logically enough, he was not a beaten enemy but a fallen hero who had fought the same adversary, the hated British.

Ben wondered who she was and what she was doing on Elba. He wondered too, but only with the faintest hope, whether he would find a chance to speak to her again.

11 Silver dollars - and brass buttons

Sir Henry, presented with two finished sketches before dinner, seemed well pleased with them. His taste, Ben had long privately decided, was not critical. The chief points he singled out for praise were the uniform of the sentries and the accurate detail of the new Elban flag, which had apparently been designed by Napoleon himself, taking the old red and silver standard of the Medici and adding the three golden bees that were among his own personal emblems.

Sir Henry had something else on his mind. Handing back the drawings, he remarked with a frown: 'Met an extraordinary woman just now.'

'Indeed, sir?'

'Quite extraordinary. American.'

Ben tried hard to hide his reaction. 'American, sir?'

'Yes. Seemed to hold me personally responsible for the burning of her President's house. Didn't know we had done. Very glad to hear it. Serve 'em right.' Sir Henry's views on Americans were uncompromising. When he was a boy, he had heard that they were disloyal rebels. Forty years later, he saw no reason to change his opinion.

'They would feel it very keenly,' Ben suggested.

'She was a dam' fool female,' said Sir Henry. 'Very ill-bred, tackling a perfect stranger like that. Gad, if she'd been a man, she'd have felt my horsewhip!' It was perhaps as well, thought Ben, that they had left the whip in Paris. 'At least her husband showed some decent embarrassment – he tried to restrain her.'

'She – has – a husband, then?' said Ben haltingly.

'Oh, yes. They landed off a ship from Leghorn this morning. I'd barely finished my breakfast.'

An obvious thought occurred to Ben. Making an excuse, he slipped from the room. His few months as a servant had taught him many useful little things. It was easy to get hold of the hotel register and glance down the freshly-written entries. Below half-a-dozen French and Italian names he read:

'Matthew Cooper, merchant, Salem, Massachusetts.
Martha Cooper, wife of the above.'

And beneath them, again:

'Fanny Blackwood, Salem, Mass.'

The last entry made him feel more cheerful, though he could not, with any sensible reason, have said why.

The inn was a homely establishment. Portferraio had seldom seen a foreign visitor until the Emperor had been brought by a British frigate eight months ago. At dinner everyone squeezed round the same long table.

The French and Italians, not conscious of any important difference between English and American, courteously held back with smiles and gestures implying that the two parties would naturally wish to sit together. They looked mystified when the American ladies pointedly ignored Sir Henry and Ben, swept down the room and took their places at the far end. Sir Henry grunted and enthroned himself at the head of the table, with Ben on his right. The rest of the company burst into a babble of talk as they scraped back the chairs and occupied the middle ground.

Glancing along, between the bobbing heads and gesticulating hands, the wine-flagons and the baskets of oranges, Ben studied the Americans as best he could.

The girl in violet, Miss Fanny Blackwood, was even more striking now that he could take her in more calmly. And even more attractive, because she was no longer haughty and indignant but laughing vivaciously as she chattered to her companions and to the Italians on the other side of her. Being Italians, they were already at her feet. What a profile, thought Ben! What a cameo she would make, with those tendrils of dark hair that had previously been half hidden under her bonnet! And equally worthy of the largest canvas too . . . How old Linfoot would have pounced upon her – with, of course, the purest of artistic motives! In his mind's eye he could see next year's Academy . . . *Portrait of Miss Fanny Blackwood, of Salem.* Linfoot would doubtless prefer her as a Grecian nymph, but would this young lady ever pose in such a capacity?

Very different was Mrs Cooper, a plump fortyish little pudding of a woman, with a strident vulgar voice and an emphatic jabbing finger. Mr Cooper, who had followed the ladies meekly, was lean, stooping and sandy-whiskered. Ben did not hear him speak. He opened his mouth only to take in the macaroni soup and the tunnyfish, the boiled fowl and the tough so-called beefsteak with its fried potatoes and onions.

Miss Blackwood was not only quite fluent in Italian, she could make spirited retorts to the Frenchmen who called compliments to her down the table. The Coopers seemed to know no language but their own. Miss Blackwood interpreted and was the centre of the lively scene. Her looks would have guaranteed that in any case.

A lady of culture, Ben deduced. Probably wealthy. An orphaned heiress, making the grand tour with these older friends. She did not call them 'Aunt' or 'Uncle', but used their surname.

At dinner she was still full of her recent encounter with the Emperor.

'It was the colour of my dress,' Ben heard her explain. 'He said he felt he must speak to me – he was sure I must wish him well.'

'And what did *you* say, Fanny?'

'That I did, indeed! I said I shared the general wish – that the Emperor would return in the spring, like the violets. I told him we had heard the saying everywhere we had been – that violet was the fashionable colour, and that everyone was wearing it to show their sympathies.'

Listening, Ben realized how blindly one travelled when one did not know the language spoken around one. Of course! That was why he had seen so many women wearing violet. He remembered the ribbon on Pierre's watch – and others he had seen. Always the same colour. All these misguided people, sharing an impossible political dream – that somehow, soon, when spring returned bringing the violets, the exile would come back to reclaim his empire and lead his armies again.

For the first time he heard Mr Cooper's gravelly but amiable voice. 'And what else did you talk about?'

'Oh, America! He is a great admirer of America! You know, Mr Cooper, he's such a *wonderful* man – I shall never forget that conversation as long as I live.'

'I hope we shall not have to listen to much more of this,' said Sir Henry very loudly and distinctly, so as to be heard the whole length of the table. ' 'Pon my soul, Ben, it makes me want to spew.'

Ben was much relieved to get through the meal without this or any other spectacular upset.

Sir Henry had been invited to take an afternoon drive with the Commissioner. Left to his own devices, Ben wandered off with his sketchbook. It was a mild day, and by finding a sheltered spot, warmed by the sun, he was able to work in comfort.

He worked fast, and with inspiration. It was the first time for months that he had felt wholly free. It was more like the old days in London, when he had roved Thames-side or Hampstead Heath with no thought but the pure pleasure of wielding his pencil. But now, with more practice, he felt a new sense of mastery.

He finished a view of the bay, with the forts and the Emperor's villa in the distance, the hills climbing behind. Then, without leaving his nook, he turned seawards, where the British brig lay at anchor and the fishing-boats made a bristling hedge of bare masts along the quays. As he completed his second sketch, a long shadow fell momentarily across the paper, then slid hastily back with a murmured apology.

He glanced up. It was Mr Cooper, a timid smile stretched between his sandy side-whiskers.

'I disturb you, sir?'

'Not at all.' Ben stood up and bowed.

'I would like to explain – Mrs Cooper's unfriendly behaviour. She feels keenly about the war. My business has suffered – some of our vessels, you understand, taken by the British Navy—'

'I am sorry, sir.'

'It is hardly your fault. And I reckon it is war. But it will not go on for ever. Our countries will do better to be friends. The ladies, of course, have a mighty admiration for this Bonaparte. I can't say I altogether go along with them in that. I figure that if he had beaten Britain and Russia, he would sooner or later have cast his eyes across the Atlantic.'

'I'm sure you're right, sir,' said Ben politely.

'You and I have no cause to quarrel—'

'Indeed, no!'

'May I examine your sketches? Thank you. I know nothing of art, Mr – er—'

'Reeth, sir.'

'Mrs Cooper is the one for art. And Miss Blackwood, of course. Mrs Cooper is set on our renting one of these palaces in Venice for the early summer. But I say, Naples first. I want to see that volcano,' Mr Cooper explained in a tone of unusual determination. 'The wonders of Nature – that's what I can appreciate. I had enough art in Rome to last a lifetime. But I mean no offence, Mr Reeth,' he added quickly, holding out the sketchbook at arm's length and examining each picture in turn. 'I reckon these are real good. A sight better than they were pushing at us all the time in Rome!'

'You're too kind.' But Ben could not help feeling pleased.

The American turned and surveyed him solemnly. 'You'll not take this amiss? You're an artist. I presume you sell your work? I'd be vastly obliged if you'd part with these two sketches. Otherwise, I guess Elba will be just a gap in Mrs Cooper's collection.'

Ben was taken aback. 'Oh – they're of no value. If you like them, pray accept them as a friendly token—'

'Quite impossible. I can't praise a man's work and then let him give it me. Oh, no.' Now that he was on more familiar commercial ground, Mr Cooper could be quite decisive. Mr Reeth must accept at least as much as he had paid for similar sketches that had taken his wife's fancy in Rome. A purse was produced. 'These Spanish dollars all right? They're worth as much as our United States dollars.' The silver pieces of eight were methodically counted out. Ben made no further attempt to refuse them. To receive the equivalent of several English guineas, for an hour or two's work that had been sheer enjoyment! He wished Linfoot could have been there to see. He had sold a picture! No, two!

'I've disturbed you long enough,' said Mr Cooper. 'We shall meet again. I *hope*,' he added doubtfully. 'I fear your friend doesn't cotton to us Yankees. And my good wife has a powerful prejudice against old titles and suchlike. Myself, I like to get along with all folks.'

'And I, sir!' Ben agreed warmly, thinking of Miss Blackwood.

Indeed, he thought of her a good deal when Mr Cooper had gone. The light was failing, but in any case he was in no mood to start a fresh drawing. He made his way back to the inn. How long, he wondered, were the Americans staying? He should have taken his chance to ask. For that matter, how long would Sir Henry want to stay before the usual restlessness drove him on?

To that question the answer came promptly, and it was one that cast Ben into gloom. Sir Henry returned from his drive in the worst of tempers.

'That fellow's an incompetent fool! Or worse.'

'Sir Neil, sir?'

'Who else? He's not fit to watch a kettle. Much less a prisoner like Boney. Who's as artful as a cageful of monkeys! I blame the government. They should have shut him up somewhere. In chains. 'Stead of that, they let him lord it here and play at being a king! Yet Sir Neil won't say a word against him. I think he positively *likes* Boney. They get on. Scandalous!'

'Was anything more said about your meeting him yourself, sir?'

Sir Henry snorted. 'It's just as I said. Sir Neil was very smooth, but he's determined to block it. Seems to think I wouldn't know how to behave myself.'

'I can't imagine why, sir.' Ben had to keep his face turned away, as he brushed Sir Henry's coat.

'It's damnably insulting! I know for a fact that a dozen English visitors have been taken to see Boney. I'll not stand it, Ben. After we've had some supper, you can pack.'

'Pack, sir?' faltered Ben.

'What is there to stay for? I've seen enough of this confounded island. We drove all over it this afternoon. Find out what time there's a boat crossing in the morning.'

'Very good, sir.' Ben knew it was useless to argue. 'And where are we going next, sir? I shall have to make inquiries – make arrangements—'

'We'll have a look at Rome.' Sir Henry did not sound particularly enthusiastic, so Ben seized his opportunity. 'You don't think you would prefer Naples, sir?'

'Naples? Why Naples?'

'It's very beautiful by all accounts. And – and there's Vesuvius—'

'Hang Vesuvius! And hang Naples! Murat is still King of Naples. They've left him in power. Scandalous! Boney's own brother-in-law – an innkeeper's son. Should have been kicked out, same time as Boney himself! I blame the government. Soft. If you think I'm going to stay in Naples, and see that jumped-up scoundrel lolling on the throne he usurped—'

'I thought, sir, that Murat came over to our side – that he broke with Bonaparte after the Battle of Leipzig—'

'I don't trust him. I don't trust any of them a yard. We shall have more trouble with them yet. Mark my words,' said Sir Henry darkly.

So the dream of Naples receded. Hitherto, it had always been Rome to which Ben had tried to direct his master's mind, so he was in no position to dissuade him now.

They did not see the American trio again. Sir Henry vowed he would not sit through supper listening to the clack of those insufferable Yankee rebels. So they ate late, and avoided another encounter. There was a boat crossing to the mainland early the next morning, and Sir Henry insisted that they should catch it.

Overnight, his fertile imagination had evolved a new fantasy. In this island of spies and secret agents even the Americans were not what they seemed. If the Emperor were to escape from Elba, where would he find a safer refuge than in the United States? It was obvious. The Coopers, and the young woman with them, must be playing a part in some dastardly plan.

Once more, Ben felt the strain of not being able to argue with his employer on equal terms. He had to keep his mouth shut, but rebelliously.

Sir Henry's suspicions of the American tourists were as wildly absurd as so many of his ideas. His estimate of Napoleon was almost equally far off the mark. Although Ben had seen the Emperor at close quarters for only a few moments, the impression had been strong. That face was not the face of a man who would run from his enemies. He would not make for America, going to earth like a fox.

As they followed the baggage-porter along the quay in the first rusty beams of the sunrise, they passed the vessel which had brought the Americans from Leghorn the previous day. The last of the cargo was being unloaded. A wooden box had just been dropped too heavily on the paving stones. It had burst open, and a little stream of what looked – from a distance – like gold coins had run jingling across the quay.

One, rolling further than the others, glittered at Ben's feet. He bent to pick it up, then smiled at his mistake – this was no gold coin but only a brass button. Even so, instinctively, just as he would have done if it had been really a guinea or a napoleon, he started towards the men unloading the cargo and held out the button. But they waved it away with a scornful laugh, saying something in Italian which he took to mean, 'Keep it – there are thousands!' And thousands there obviously were. So, without pressing the matter, he slipped the button into his pocket as a souvenir.

It was hours later when, groping for money, he fished out the button and looked at it properly. It was an ordinary brass button, such as soldiers wore on their tunics and greatcoats. It was brand new – and it bore an eagle.

Under that emblem Bonaparte's armies had conquered Europe. But in his exile their leader no longer used it: it was the bee, not the eagle, that he had chosen for the Elban flag.

Why were thousands of new eagle buttons being delivered to him here? The question kept recurring in Ben's mind as the diligence trundled through Tuscany along the road to Rome.

12 At the Spanish Steps

The journey was uneventful, apart from a little trouble between Sir Henry and a customs officer at the frontier of the Pope's dominions. Arrived in Rome, they found a good hotel in the Via della Croce, in the quarter recommended to British tourists. At the end of the street, beyond a square with a curious fountain, an elaborate double staircase, the Spanish Steps, climbed the hill to a twin-towered church that stood out against the sky. The steps were crowded with flower-sellers, peasant girls in gold brocaded petticoats and scarlet stockings, sitting by huge baskets of spring blooms. The scent from those baskets carried Ben back to Covent Garden. More than once, too, the bold-eyed girls reminded him of Sal. Otherwise, he seldom thought of her now.

Sir Henry set himself to view the wonders of Rome with his customary energy.

'You'd better find us one of these guide fellows,' he instructed Ben. 'What do they call 'em – a *cicerone*?'

'Yes, sir.'

'Have him here first thing tomorrow morning. With a chaise. Four horses.'

'Four, sir? Some of these streets seem rather narrow. And the traffic is—'

'Four,' said Sir Henry firmly. 'I want to get round. See all there is to see. But quickly.'

So they embarked upon a whirlwind programme of sight-seeing. The guide, Luigi, and the driver, Matteo, made a quick estimate of Sir Henry's character – and the depth of his purse. Everything, promised Luigi, should be as the milord wished.

It was lucky, thought Ben, that they were not attempting this in the heat of a Roman summer. Even so, it was exhausting.

Famous statues and fountains, palaces and villas, pagan monuments from the days of the Caesars and churches dating from the early centuries of Christianity – Sir Henry was determined to see everything.

Luigi learned to cut short the explanations. Sir Henry liked to leap out of his carriage, cover the ground in a few brisk strides, cock his head this way and that like a questing bird, rap out a comment, and be off again.

It was Ben's duty to jot down what they had seen, keeping the record up to date as the chaise raced headlong through the streets, up and down the famous seven hills of Rome, scattering urchins and crippled beggars and dozing dogs as it went.

He suspected that Sir Henry, after the first dozen buildings visited, enjoyed the sightseeing less than the excitement of the driving between.

'I won't say it licks steeple-chasing,' panted his master, bracing himself as they swept perilously round a sharp corner, 'but it comes near it.' He grinned. 'Same idea, after all! When we go steeple-chasing we pick some church in the distance, and make for it, hell-for-leather, across country. Can't quite do that here – and these churches don't seem to go in for steeples – but it's good sport, all the same.'

At dinner on the second day Ben attempted a gentle protest.

'But you're not really *seeing* anything, sir! Not to take it in. You won't remember it.'

Sir Henry flushed. 'You're keeping your list, aren't you?'

'Yes, sir.'

'Well then!'

'A list of pictures and statues and ancient ruins – it's *only* a list. It's – it's the difference between reading this bill of fare and eating the actual meal. You have to look at things slowly and quietly, digest what you see—'

'Are you telling me what to do?' demanded Sir Henry in a danger-laden voice.

'Certainly not, sir. It's merely that—'

'I know what I'm doing. Why does a man tour Italy? To be able to *say* that he has seen this place and that. I know what it will be when I get back to England. Simpering females cross-examining me like schoolmarms! "Surely you saw the frescoes in St Thingummy's? But why not? And you never visited the Villa Marconi? But *why*?" I'll not put up with it. I have calculated,' Sir Henry concluded grandly, 'that if the ordinary tourist can cover the sights in six weeks, I can do it in one. And I'll remember as much as he does.'

Or as little, thought Ben.

One possible consolation occurred to him. If Sir Henry exhausted the attractions of Rome at this pace, he would soon move on. Then perhaps it would be possible to revive, tactfully, the suggestion of Naples. Surely to a man of Sir Henry's volcanic temperament there would be an attraction in Vesuvius?

Ben himself had always had a strong desire to view that remarkable mountain and the bay of legendary beauty curving at its feet. But the particular appeal of Naples, at this moment, he would not have confessed to anyone.

Indeed, he would hardly admit it to himself. Suppose he

prevailed on Sir Henry to visit Naples. Suppose – and this seemed unlikeliest of all – that both parties forgot their Anglo-American hostility and became normally civil to each other.

It would make no difference. Miss Blackwood was a grand young lady, obviously rich – how else could she make this leisurely tour of Europe? And what was he? Not even a poor artist. Barely even a proper valet, 'a gentleman's gentleman'. To Miss Blackwood, if she ever knew the full truth, he would be only a workman.

Ben had watched many a sentimental romance as he stood in the wings at Covent Garden, but he knew that what the fashionable audience clapped in the theatre they would never allow to happen in real life.

None the less, absurd, hopeless and illogical as it all was, he felt a stubborn desire to see that girl again if ever he could make the opportunity.

Sir Henry, of course, was just as likely to charge off in the opposite direction. More likely.

From time to time he dropped wistful references to the establishment he had abandoned so abruptly in Paris. He wondered how things were at the château. Was Jupp coping with Pierre and all those thievish mounseers? Were the horses being kept in sound condition? He never mentioned the gorgeous Georgina, but Ben did not imagine that she was forgotten. He steeled himself for Sir Henry's instructions, any day now: pack for Paris.

They did not come. After a time he realized why.

Sir Henry was a proud man. He had made his gesture, his grand exit. He would not crawl back to Lady Mulroy with his tail between his legs. She must make the first move.

'Take these to the post-office.'

With a grunt of relief, for he disliked writing, Sir Henry sanded the ink, sealed the last letter, and thrust it into Ben's hand with three others. Two were for London, addressed to his bankers and his man of business there. Two were directed to the château, to Jupp and Lord Mulroy.

'We'll need to stay in Rome for a few weeks, Ben. Give 'em time to reply.'

It was childishly obvious. Without writing to her ladyship, Sir Henry was ensuring that she knew his whereabouts. It was open to her now either to plead with him to return or to inform him that the Mulroys too were starting for Rome.

Ben would never have expected Sir Henry to have the patience for a waiting game, but, once the strenuous sight-seeing was over, he was finding plenty of amusement.

Rome was full of British tourists, and the better sort stayed mostly in this quarter below the Spanish Steps. Sir Henry was continually meeting ladies and gentlemen of his acquaintance. This led to fresh introductions and frequent invitations. The Corso, the broad thoroughfare running straight across the other end of their street, seemed almost as English as Piccadilly. When Sir Henry took his stroll at the fashionable hour, his hat was more often in his hand than on his head.

Ben, needless to say, had no part in this new social life, with its rides and drives and dinner-parties and opera-going. Nor was he required to accompany Sir Henry on his long evenings with the other gentlemen, playing cards or billiards or simply drinking. His role was confined to helping Sir Henry to bed, lugging off his boots and peeling the tight-stretched breeches from his ample thighs.

He had become once more the valet, or more vaguely 'my man'.

It was to be expected. On the long road from Paris, sharing rooms in wayside inns or wedged knee to knee in a diligence all night and all day, they would have found it impossible to maintain the gulf between master and servant. But that free-and-easy intimacy was behind them now. Ben did not mind.

All the same, those weeks in Rome were not without their irritations.

Sometimes, observing Sir Henry with his friends, he was almost ashamed of being English. Their lordly manners, their loud voices, their cackling laughter, drew every eye upon them. They were so *superior*, the men with their trim London tailoring, cravats and canes, the ladies buttoned up in their long mannish redingotes, with their hats like officers' helmets and their ostrich-plumes. With what arrogance they surveyed the local population, who had the three-fold misfortune to be Italians, Catholics, and poor!

The English were certainly not poor. They scattered their money thoughtlessly, so that the beggars converged like wasps in summer. Sir Henry had only to step round to his Roman banker, and, on signature, the gold would stream as though it were jingling down a pipe laid straight from London. His new cronies seemed just as comfortably provided. Mr Apperley owned vast sugar-estates in Jamaica and old Sir Rupert Dodds had brought home a fortune from Bengal. Lord Frederick Baslow had once eloped with an heiress, gained control of her wealth, as the law allowed, and now seemed to be getting rid of it very quickly, though not as quickly as he had got rid of her.

It seemed all wrong.

At times Ben came near to hating Sir Henry.

He would stand patiently behind him, waiting for orders, staring at the gross folds of flesh on his neck. Late nights, heavy eating and deep drinking had improved neither Sir Henry's health nor his temper. His present friends, Ben decided, were not good for him. He was more than ever like a spoilt child, finding fault and flying into a passion. Ben was often reminded of the way he had bullied the servants on the Southampton pier.

Thank Heaven, they were apart much of the day! Ben had time on his hands, to explore Rome at his own pace and obey Linfoot's injunction to 'study the antique'.

There were sketches to be made for Sir Henry, obvious subjects such as the dome of St Peter's seen across the Tiber, the stupendous broken shell of the Colosseum, and the Castel Sant' Angelo, like a giant's cake with battlements. Sir Henry had an understandable taste for the outsize.

These done, Ben was free to follow his own preferences. He liked the smaller subjects, some quiet corner with one graceful ruined column or a cypress, a lesser fountain with rollicking dolphins or sly cupids. As he gained in confidence, he turned from bronze and marble to figures of flesh and blood. Donkeys in carts and glossy carriage-horses, bedraggled beggars and picturesque Papal Guards, elderly friars and skittish flower-girls: all went into his sketchbook.

Not all remained there. Tourists would pause. Some, usually the British, would ask if his work was for sale. He always said yes. Money had never come easily in the Reeth family. Let it come now! He could always do more sketches. He sold cheaply, sometimes he thought perhaps too cheaply. He was still surprised that he could earn money by doing what he enjoyed. Even so, his private savings began to accumulate.

Time and again he returned to the Spanish Steps. They were near the hotel, ideal for spare hours when he dared not be absent too long. His favourite place was at the very top, with the street and church behind him and the western skyline, with the Vatican and the long Janiculum ridge, stretched out in front.

There was always so much life and movement there. People streamed up and down like the angels on Jacob's Ladder, endlessly. There were a hundred and thirty-seven steps. He had counted them. If he saw an interesting character toiling up, he could rely on that person pausing for a few moments at the top. There was usually time for at least a lightning sketch.

Frankly too, as he had heard men say in Covent Garden Market, it was a good pitch. He sold several sketches there.

He would have sold another – but for Sir Henry. An interested German tourist was already hovering at his elbow, but the drawing was fated to remain in the book, with Ben's methodical note, *'Unfinished Flower Girl, Rome, Feb 14, 1815.'* Suddenly Sir Henry exploded behind them.

'You young devil! So it's true!'

Ben sprang to his feet and turned. Sir Henry was just dismounting from Lord Frederick's crested carriage, which had pulled up in front of the church door. Lord Frederick and Sir Rupert Dodds were watching amusedly.

'I beg your pardon, sir. You were requiring me?'

'I was told I'd likely find you here. Gad, a servant of mine! Hawking goods in the street like a cheapjack! My friends will be asking, don't I pay you enough?'

Ben flushed. 'I am sorry, sir, if I have done anything to displease you—'

'Displease? Blast you, boy, you've dam' near given me an apoplexy! Never so shamed in all my life.' Sir Henry thrust out a roll of paper. His hand was shaking with fury. 'Is this yours? Or ain't it?'

Ben unrolled the sketch. He saw his own initials, the date, and title. '*Sleeping Beggar by Triton Fountain.*' He had sold it to an English lady five days before. He handed it back.

'Yes, sir. It's mine, of course. May I ask how you—'

'I bought it, you dog. Bought it back from a lady who showed it to me just now. What else could I do? My own servant! What the devil do you mean by it? What right have you—'

'I've surely a right to do what I choose in my free time—'

'Not *this*!' howled Sir Henry. 'I employ you. Any drawing you do, you do for me. As I instruct you.'

'With respect, sir, no.'

'What? What? Don't presume to argue with me!'

Ben stood his ground. 'I've sketched everything you asked for. After that, I shall do as I please with my own work.'

'You will? Don't try that line with me! You've got above yourself, you rogue. I shall do as *I* please with this trash!' Sir Henry held up the sketch in both hands for all to see – and by this time, besides Lord Frederick and Sir Rupert grinning in the background, quite a crowd had gathered to goggle at the quarrelling Englishmen. Gazing about him with a malicious smirk, Sir Henry very deliberately tore the paper across, shredded it into smaller pieces, and sent those pieces scudding like snowflakes down the steps.

This was too much for Ben. For six months he had controlled himself under every provocation. He had reached the limit. He gave Sir Henry a clout on the ear that sent him staggering.

There was something like a cheer from the bystanders. Even the poorest and most illiterate Italian seemed to have a respect for the artist.

The cheer did not improve Sir Henry's temper, already boiling over. 'You insufferable scoundrel! You need a lesson!'

He snatched the whip from the hand of Lord Frederick's driver, who was hurrying to his aid. The crowd fell back hastily as Sir Henry advanced balefully, making a broad sweep which gave everyone ample time to foresee his alarming intentions.

Ben was no slower than the others. This emergency called for something more decisive than a second box on the ear. He hit out as he had once hit out at a drunken porter in the market.

Sir Henry took the blow square on the chin. He rocked on his heels, then stumbled over the top step, and went sprawling down. The flower-girls squealed and scattered. The wicker baskets toppled and rolled, bumping at every step and scattering their blooms. On a fragrant stair-carpet of crushed spring flowers Sir Henry slid and tumbled ignominiously until he came to rest against the balustrade.

13 'Liberty - and the pursuit of happiness'

Ben was quite prepared for instant dismissal. Indeed, he would not have been surprised if he had been handed over at once to the police and left to spend the night in some unsavoury dungeon.

In the end, as he was glad to admit, Sir Henry behaved uncommonly well.

'Of course, you'll have to go,' he announced when they

faced each other in his room an hour or two later. Yet there was a note of reluctance in his voice.

Ben felt pretty sure that if Sir Henry's humiliation had not been so public the whole affair might have blown over. No man had ever before knocked Sir Henry down, and, blustering bully though he was, he had enough sporting spirit to admire anyone who could. But two of his grand friends had seen his undignified descent of the Spanish Steps, and he knew how quickly the story would run round the British tourists in Rome. Ben realized that Sir Henry could not face his friends and confess that his valet was still in his employ.

That understood, Sir Henry bore no grudge.

Ben's back wages were paid up to date. 'And I must give you something for the journey back to England,' growled Sir Henry. 'Whatever the rights and wrongs, I can't let it be said I turned off a servant in the middle of nowhere.'

'There is no need, sir. I shall not be going home immediately. And—' Ben checked a smile— 'I have other resources.'

'The devil you have!' Sir Henry grinned sheepishly. 'Well, good luck to you, you young scamp.' A thought struck him. 'I'll give you a reference if you ever need one – though I'll need to phrase it carefully. But I've a notion you'll not look for a post as valet again.'

'So have I, sir!' Ben accepted a paper, however, stating that he had left Sir Henry's service by mutual agreement. It was best to have it, lest he were ever suspected of being a runaway. He also remembered to ask for his passport.

It was good to hold the document in his own hand. *Benjamin Reeth* .. He was an individual again, free to go where he liked. What was that eloquent American phrase? 'Life, liberty, and the pursuit of happiness.' He had liberty now. Pursuit . . .?

If he needed an omen, it came with the English newspapers that arrived in a great batch that very evening. Some were stale – there had been a delay to mail passing through Savoy. After weeks of ignorance, however, even old news seemed fresh.

At Christmas a treaty had been signed at Ghent. The war

between Britain and America was over. It had been over, though they had not known it, even when they were on Elba. So, if he met Miss Blackwood again – a big 'if', alas – they need not meet as enemies.

Next morning he went early to the police station to show his passport. Thence he was sent on to the city governor, to get it endorsed for Naples. This involved a tiresome wait and a bribe to a clerk. After that he had almost to run to the Neapolitan consulate, to get a counter-signature before the office shut for the siesta.

After dinner he found a *vetturino*, an independent coach-driver, starting for Naples on the morrow. Eager to fill the fourth seat, he agreed to take Ben for ten Spanish dollars. 'Meals and beds included, *signore* – everything.'

'How far is it?'

The Italian rolled his eyes. 'It is a long journey. We arrive, God willing, on the fifth day.'

'Five days!' Ben had an idea that the distance was about a hundred and thirty miles.

'We do not travel in the dark, *signore*. For fear of bandits. Each night you sleep at a good inn, with dinner, wine, everything of the best. Four nights! God knows why I do it. Only ten dollars! I ruin myself.'

'I am sure you do,' said Ben.

He was careful to get a receipt. He had just about enough Italian to check that it was in order.

It was soon clear, next day, why the journey took so long. The road, good in some stretches, was appalling in others. The horses were of miserable quality, and the *vetturino* treated them, in one respect at least, as he did his passengers; he did not overfeed them.

At any other time Ben might have appreciated the leisurely pace, so slow that often he and another passenger, a German doctor who spoke some English, preferred to get out and walk a few miles. He would have welcomed the chance to take in the views, which varied from the volcanic shapes of the Alban Hills on their left to the luxuriant malarial jungle which stretched on their right towards the sea. Spring was unfurling everywhere.

Ben was not, however, in the mood to contemplate scenery. A powerful impulse – foolish, he tried to tell himself, and quite irrational – was driving him to Naples. He sighed for the speed of an English mail-coach, flashing along a fine turn-pike behind a glossy team. He even thought wistfully of those exhausting all-night journeys in the diligence lumbering across France and Switzerland.

Suppose the Americans had left Naples by now? His one comfort was the knowledge that they had been planning to go on to Venice for the summer – and in Rome everyone had assured him that Venetian weather was vile until April.

Well, if they had gone from Naples, they had gone. He shrugged his shoulders at the thought, trying to convince him-self that he was indifferent – and entirely failing to do so. When he turned homewards, he would probably visit Venice. That was only sensible. No Englishman would miss Venice. Whether or not he chanced to meet the Americans there was purely incidental.

He grinned suddenly, seeing through his own hypocrisy. The German doctor stared anxiously, as though suspecting some mental defect.

After their second night, spent on the coast at Terracina, they entered the Kingdom of Naples, and their progress if anything grew slower. There was a long delay at the frontier with much scrutiny of baggage and passports. After that, there were frequent checks along the road. They saw troops posted at intervals, questioning travellers.

'I suppose it's because of the bandits?' Ben suggested.

'Not entirely,' said the German. 'It is the general political uncertainty.' There were two parties, he explained. One backed Murat, whom the Allies had so far left on his throne as a reward for deserting Napoleon. The other party wanted to bring back the lawful king, who still held the Sicilian half of his territories, reigning in Palermo with British help. So Murat was nervous, and kept this firm military grip on the mainland. 'Also,' concluded the German solemnly, 'we must ask ourselves – as Murat must ask himself – is it *certain* we have finished with Napoleon?'

Ben murmured politely. It was not a question that worried him.

That day, their third, they drove between endless orange groves with warm golden fruit, startling white blossom, and brightly shining leaves. For the first time they reached the sea. They slept at a little port called Gaeta, where the beauty of the view took Ben's breath away. Beyond the hills to the south there was a glimpse of Vesuvius, trailing a smoke-plume across a fiery sunset sky.

That was the best day. Mostly the journey was tiresome. The wretched horses crept like snails. The passengers had to battle continually with the *vetturino* to secure decent beds and eatable meals. The innkeepers were insolent and indifferent, since it was the *vetturino* who paid the bill, and he, having already pocketed the fares, grudged every penny. If Ben and his companions had not disputed every detail, they would have been crowded into the worst bedroom and given a sort of prison diet, washed down with the sourest wine.

There was only one more night, at Capua. Everyone was heartily thankful when, on the fifth afternoon, they saw Naples, outspread like some giant fan around its famous bay.

Ben was daunted for a few minutes by the sheer size of the place, seen like this from the surrounding hills. Here was a royal capital, one of the busiest Mediterranean ports, a human anthill – in which he hoped to find one girl. Then, as they creaked down the last dusty mile, his determination revived.

He had seen other great cities. Foreign tourists were usually to be found in one or two favourite quarters. It would be the same in Naples. He could disregard this rabbit-warren of sinister alleys opening off to left and right. The Coopers' hotel would not be in the slums.

It would be more difficult, of course, if they had taken lodgings or rented a house. Foreigners were apt to do that when making a lengthy stay. He remembered thankfully that there would be an American consul. Mr Cooper, with his commercial and shipping interests, would never pass through Naples without paying a courtesy call.

Ben parted from the *vetturino* without regret. The German knew an inexpensive little inn, so they shared a baggage-porter and went there together. The next morning, as soon as Ben had redeemed his passport from the police, he made for the waterfront and looked for the house from whose balcony fluttered the Stars and Stripes.

The consul received him with guarded cordiality.

'I can shake your hand, Mr Reeth – as I could scarcely have done a few weeks ago. The war's over and we can be civil again. But I'm puzzled – you have your own British consul – you should go to Mr Walker.'

'I think, sir, you may be able to help me more – if you will.'

At the name Cooper the atmosphere cleared. 'Of course! Mr Cooper has been at the Hotel Crocelle since the end of January.' The consul told Ben which way to go, and five minutes later he was striding through the streets.

Now that the moment had come, a sudden nervousness swept over him. But surely, he told himself, it would be permissible to call and pay his respects? After all, Mr Cooper had bought two of his sketches. Their countries were no longer at war. Sir Henry was not here to make trouble. It was all most reasonable. None the less, he was licking his lips and silently rehearsing what he would say.

Something was happening outside the Hotel Crocelle. Even from a distance he could tell that. An open carriage was drawn up in front. A crowd of beggars had appeared from nowhere. The German had warned him about the notorious Neopolitan rabble, the tattered and tattooed *lazzaroni*. Over their heads Ben saw hotel servants lifting things into the vehicle. Then came a glimpse of a woman's bonnet, rising, tilting and subsiding again, as its wearer mounted and took her seat. A second bonnet followed, then a top hat. The driver cracked his whip and the horses started forward. They came towards Ben, scattering the beggars to right and left.

By the time the carriage passed him it was bowling along at a smart pace. The driver was twirling his whip to discourage the more persistent *lazzaroni* who raced alongside with outstretched palms. Ben had to step out of their way to avoid a collision.

Thus he was able to get only a fleeting impression of the ladies in the carriage. But there was no mistaking the round red face of Mrs Cooper. Nor the slim dark girl laughing beside her. She was in a white dress today but with a fichu round her shoulders – of violet.

14 The picnic

He conquered an impulse to turn and race after them. Instead, hurrying forward to the hotel, he caught a disappearing porter.

'The Americani!' he cried urgently. 'My friends,' he added hastily as the little man gaped up at him. He fumbled to phrase his question in Italian. To what city were they departing?

No city, it seemed. The porter had some English and he now changed to that language. 'They come back, *signore*,' he said reassuringly. 'They not leave Naples.'

'But they had baggage! I saw it.'

'No, no, *signore*. Baskets only. The Americani take their dinner to the mountain.'

'A picnic?'

The word puzzled the Italian. 'No, no, *signore*. On the mountain. Alfresco!'

'Same thing,' said Ben impatiently. 'Which mountain?'

'Vesuvio, *signore* – where else?'

Ben remembered Mr Cooper's special enthusiasms.

The porter said that the Americani would be back by dusk. It was only a few miles to the foot of the mountain. No distance. No, himself, he had never been.

Ben tipped him, much relieved, and declined his offer to call a carriage. He could see the mountain, the way was obvious, and the walk would calm his restless mood. He had had enough of these hired vehicles and the haggling over terms. He would never overtake the Coopers in that dashing carriage and four, but once on the mountain it would be a different matter.

It was as warm as a summer's day at home. The narrow, poker-straight cypresses barely striped the road with shade. The orchards offered even less, though the apple and almond trees were clouds of white and pink blossom. The vines in their straight green rows gave no shelter whatever. He trudged purposefully forward, straight into the sun, beads of sweat standing out on his temples, his shirt stuck to his body.

In front Vesuvius rose faint and grey. It was hard to be sure how much was the heat-haze veiling the whole landscape, how much the vapours special to the volcano.

Mr Cooper was lucky to be visiting Naples at a time of activity. Sometimes, Ben gathered, the mountain slumbered peacefully for years on end. There had been no dramatic eruption since 1794, but at present the volcano was spitting enough smoke and flame to satisfy the tourists. What was it that the German had said last night in his cynical way? 'This is a mountain that vomits gold for the innkeepers and donkeymen.'

The Vesuvius trade was certainly well organized. When, after an hour or more's hard walking, it was time to turn off and strike up the mountainside, there was no fear of his missing the way. Half a dozen gigs and carriages were drawn up at the roadside, their drivers dozing, their horses cropping the scanty grass. There was also a line of tethered mules and donkeys, ready to be hired. Peasant-girls, gaily petticoated and shawled, squatted beside mounds of oranges and flagons of wine cooling in a runnel of water in the ditch.

There was little stir as Ben approached. Clearly, no one arriving on foot was expected to have any money. Closer view, however, must have shown that Ben was foreign. As many English milords were mad, one might even be mad enough to walk like a peasant though he could afford to ride. The girls ceased to gossip. They held out oranges and wine-bottles and made play with their long-lashed eyes. Several men converged on Ben, offering themselves as guides and their mules as transport. He brushed them aside, pausing only to buy some fruit, and started up a well-trodden path that could only lead to the summit.

The men's voices followed him, plaintive at first, then indignant and no doubt uncomplimentary. *'Pericoloso!'* they warned him.

Perilous? How absurd, he thought, fixing his eyes on the skyline. A little cavalcade was outlined against a drifting cream-white cloud. The ladies, perched on their donkeys, were holding up umbrellas to prevent sunburn. It was the only danger they seemed to fear.

This mountain was nothing compared with those awful Alps. Not much higher (he had read somewhere) than the Welsh Snowdon, and less precipitous. Just a long grind uphill. He would waste no money on mules, much less on guides.

The first stretch was between vineyards. After that came rugged expanses of rock, where streams of lava from past eruptions had congealed and petrified into odd-looking ridges. He was reminded of those pasteboard waves he had often had to fix across the stage to represent the sea.

Another party came jingling down, a British naval officer, some giggling ladies, and an elderly gentleman who called out: 'Well worth it! Phenomenal!'

It was noon now. Ben was hot and dusty. The hard rock gave place to a carpet of ash and cinders, ankle-deep. He plodded on, peeling an orange as he climbed. Yes, a long uphill grind . . .

This must be what they called the cone of the volcano. And surely that was the summit he could see? Clustered figures, some seated under umbrellas . . . Beasts standing patiently with empty saddles . . .

From time to time he could hear a low thunderous rumble. Then would come a roar like the discharge of a cannon, and from a point to one side of the summit a dark jet would shoot up into the air, hundreds of feet – a mass of sulphurous smoke and grey ash and glowing red-hot stones. He could hear the people exclaiming shrilly and see their arms pointing jerkily, like a marionette's.

He mopped his brow and his handkerchief came away grimy. As he battled his way up the last two hundred yards he identified Mrs Cooper enthroned amid the picnic-baskets and her attentive husband with a wine-bottle that flashed back the sun.

They recognized him as he drew nearer. Mr Cooper called out a genial welcome. Mrs Cooper flapped a languid hand.

'So you found your way to Naples, too?' said the merchant. 'What have you done with Sir Henry?'

Mrs Cooper broke in, acidly: 'You would scarcely expect him to walk up here! And what mule could carry him?'

Mr Cooper looked embarrassed. Ben quickly explained. He had parted company with Sir Henry and was travelling alone.

'You will share our refreshment, Mr Reeth?' inquired the merchant. 'You have heard the good news, of course? The war is over. We may sit down together now as friends.'

'Pray do,' said his wife, without undue enthusiasm.

'That's most kind, ma'am.'

Mr Cooper observed Ben's questing glance along the mountainside. 'The crater is just down there,' he said. 'The guide said—'

'He *said* it would be less smoky here for our picnic,' Mrs Cooper interrupted, 'but I declare it is all fumes and brimstone wherever one turns.'

'Perhaps you wish to see the crater first?' suggested Mr Cooper. 'Miss Blackwood said she would stay a few more minutes. Perhaps you would have the goodness to tell her we are about to eat?'

'With pleasure.' Ben went crunching his way across the mountain-top before Mrs Cooper could countermand her husband's message.

The crater lay to the south of the summit, a vast irregular greyish bowl like a quarry, some hundreds of feet deep and several hundred yards across. Beyond its further edge he could see the blue bay far below, the green plain, and a pattern of faint blobs which must be the excavations at Pompeii. At his feet, however, the slope fell away to this dead eerie landscape that might have been an illustration to Dante's *Inferno*.

A French family party was coming back, picking its way up the cindery path. Wisps of acrid smoke drifted across, slowly unravelling in the warm air. The place smelt, thought Ben, wrinkling his nose distastefully, like some gigantic ash-heap outside a factory engine-house. The French ladies had their handkerchiefs pressed to their faces.

Very far from dead was the inner crater, a much smaller hollow which, as he began his slithering descent, rumbled ominously, roared and sent up another tall plume of smoke and molten rock. This, however, was some distance away, and the sightseers were giving it a wide berth. For the most part the floor of the main crater encircling it looked safe enough, if not a particularly agreeable place to linger in. A scholarly gentleman was writing in his notebook, another was gathering lumps of pumice as souvenirs. If Ben's mind had not been on other matters, he would have got out his sketchbook and recorded the scene.

His eyes were taken, though, by a white figure picking a fastidious way across the desert of slag. The girl was much nearer to the inner crater than any of the other visitors.

One of the guides conducting another party turned and looked in her direction with obvious concern. Then he cupped his hands and sent his resonant Italian voice echoing round the rocky bowl.

'*Signorina!*'

The girl glanced back and raised a hand in acknowledgment. She must have seen Ben also, but she showed no sign of recognition.

'*Signorina!*' persisted the guide. '*Pericoloso!*'

She waved her hand again, dismissively, and continued walking towards the inner crater.

The Italian swore under his breath. He rolled his eyes at

Ben, shrugged his shoulders, and went scrambling up the slope to overtake his party.

This time Ben was less inclined to laugh at the warning. That inner crater was a positive hell's mouth. When it spat, there must be a rain of hot fragments all round it and the rush of fumes would be suffocating. No doubt Miss Blackwood was counting on a fair interval before there was another discharge, but did a volcano keep time like a clock? Ben questioned that. In any case, that smoking hole was terrifying enough in itself. Suppose she took one step too near its lip – suppose the treacherous cinders began to slide, and she went down, down—

The mere thought was unbearable. He broke into a run, so far as that was possible on the soft yielding surface underfoot. It seemed a long way. It *was* a long way.

'Miss Blackwood!' he yelled.

She paused at the sound of her own name. And in the same moment there came the threatening rumble from beneath them. She backed away now, picked up her flowing skirts and began to run. It was late, though. The mountain's warning was short. She had taken only half a dozen stumbling paces when the explosion came.

Ben heard her scream and saw her fall. Then all sight of her was blotted out by the cloud of choking, sulphurous fumes that came bellying out of the earth and rolling across the sky.

15 Eagle in flight

Blindly, spluttering in the fetid gases, Ben plunged forward. He tore off his neckcloth as he went, and tied it over his mouth and nose. Burning cinders rained down. A lump as big as a football dropped – mercifully – a yard in front of him.

His boot caught it, but it was still soft and yielding. He recovered his balance and floundered on.

The veil of dirty yellow fumes was thinning. He saw the whiteness of her dress, outspread on the grey ground. She lay face downwards, quite still.

He stooped, slipped his arms under her, and picked her up. She was no weight at all, but the deep ash made speed difficult. The air grew fresher at every stride. Now the crater-wall rose clear ahead, tourists strung along the path, transfixed with alarm.

One of the local guides waved his straw hat. *'Bravo, signore! Bravissimo!'* That started it. Every one began to shout and clap. By the time Ben reached safety, a dozen people were crowding round and congratulating him in various languages.

Miss Blackwood had recovered consciousness, if indeed she had ever entirely lost it. She stirred in Ben's arms, fluttered her eyes, and murmured: 'I am so sorry – that was so *stupid*.' He set her down gingerly, and was relieved to find that she could stand. 'Mr Reeth!' she exclaimed with every sign of astonishment. He was delighted that, even in the stress of the moment, she recalled his name. It was sharp of her, too, to recognize him before he had pulled the cloth from the lower half of his face. 'What on earth are *you* doing here?' she demanded.

That question could wait. 'Can you walk?' he said.

'If you will give me your hand.'

They took the steep path gently. She did not refuse his arm also, round her waist.

They found the Coopers growing anxious. Mrs Cooper's expression turned to one of suspicion until Miss Blackwood explained.

'Really, Fanny! You are so foolhardy. Your dress! And your face!'

'They will both wash.'

'You look like a chimney-sweep. I declare, I should never let you out of my sight.'

Mr Cooper said mildly: 'My love, Fanny is not your *child*. Or anyone else's. She is old enough to do as she pleases.'

They all seemed glad of Ben's presence, as an outsider, to relieve the strain. Mrs Cooper became cordial. She bade him sit down on of the saddle-cloths. She pressed him to cold ham and chicken, sausage and melon and other good things from the baskets brought up by the muleteer.

'This wine,' said Mr Cooper, 'comes from the grapes grown on this very mountain. *Lachryma Christi.*'

' "Tears of Christ",' the girl translated, sipping the pale golden liquid.

'Miss Blackwood is our scholar,' Mr Cooper explained.

'It is a most blasphemous name,' said his wife severely. 'It is only for health's sake that I touch wine at all.'

Mr Cooper filled Ben's glass. 'How long have you been in Naples? Had we dreamed you were coming here today, we would have stopped the carriage and turned back for you.'

Ah, thought Ben, so they saw me outside the hotel! He glanced at the girl. Her face and neck had grown suddenly pink.

Two can play at this game, he told himself. Aloud, he said blandly, 'I'd imagined you all in Venice, long ago.'

'There is so much to see,' said Mrs Cooper. 'I tell my husband, he has partners, let them take care of his business until the fall. A tour of Europe is something to last a lifetime.'

'It will have to,' said Miss Blackwood wistfully.

After what Mr Cooper insisted on calling the 'gallant rescue', it was obvious that Ben must drive back to Naples with them. The guide and muleteer gathered up the remains of the meal, the Americans mounted, and they set off. Ben led Miss Blackwood's mule, ready to help if she turned faint again, but the girl seemed remarkably full of vitality.

Then, and later during the short carriage-drive, he picked up a little more information about the trio.

Miss Blackwood was an orphan, with a married sister in Boston. Of her parentage nothing was said, and he could scarcely ask questions. The Coopers were old family friends, and, since she could not tour Europe alone, she had seized the chance to come with them.

Mrs Cooper talked about culture, Miss Blackwood possessed it. On Elba he had noted her command of French and Italian. She was well read, though not forbiddingly so, with a taste for history and literature.

He kept his end up quite well. Thanks to Linfoot, he could grasp her allusions to Virgil and Cicero. And thanks to his connections with the theatre – he did not reveal the nature of the connection – he could talk lightly about the plays and actors he had seen.

Mrs Cooper mellowed with every mile. It was so delightful to meet someone who knew Royal Academicians and had seen all the latest pieces at Covent Garden. Now that this tiresome war was over, she must prevail upon Mr Cooper to take them home by way of England.

'You must indeed!' cried Ben. Then, with some embarrassment, he remembered Somerset Alley. He remembered Sal, also. It was some time since he had thought of her. That caused him no pang of conscience, but he did feel rather guilty at allowing his new friends to develop false ideas about him.

Yet, if he spoke frankly about his humble circumstances, he knew it would finish this pleasant acquaintance as abruptly as it had begun. These Americans talked a great deal about all men being created equal, but one had only to observe Mrs Cooper, and the tone in which she commanded and upbraided the Italians waiting upon her, to realize how little she believed in the principle. If she were to guess that Ben was only a working man, she would hardly be able to tolerate his presence in the carriage.

He disliked deception. But so long as he was not forced into telling lies about himself, why force unwelcome facts upon her? This friendship would live no longer than a butterfly, anyhow. No point in killing it. Miss Blackwood seemed to be enjoying it as much as he was.

Mrs Cooper turned to her as they drew near the hotel. 'You will tell the driver, Fanny, that we require the carriage tomorrow morning?' She looked across at Ben. 'You will join us, Mr Reeth? We are going to see the King review his troops.'

Ben accepted eagerly. He would have joined in far duller entertainments if there had been no other way of meeting Miss Blackwood again. But in fact it was a delightful enough way to pass a sunny spring morning, seated in the carriage or standing beside it, while five thousand cavalry and infantry made multi-coloured patterns on the parade-ground to the stirring music of a dozen bands.

They had a good view of Murat. Even Mrs Cooper had to admit that he looked every inch a king, though his father had been only an innkeeper. He must by now be in his late forties, for he had been one of Napoleon's officers from the earliest days, but whereas the Emperor had put on weight with the years Murat still rode his charger like the dashing colonel of chasseurs who had led his men at the Battle of the Pyramids. 'He is so good-looking,' sighed Mrs Cooper.

'But untrustworthy,' said Miss Blackwood. 'He marries Napoleon's sister – and then he deserts Napoleon, simply to keep his crown. The crown Napoleon gave him!'

'Well, Napoleon's sister looks remarkably happy,' Ben pointed out, looking towards the royal carriage, from which the Queen of Naples was smiling and waving to her husband.

'Murat may change sides again,' said Mr Cooper shrewdly. 'If it proves worth his while.'

Ben noted, however, that no Bonapartist sympathizers were flaunting their colours in this fashionable crowd. Even Miss Blackwood had left her violet scarf at the hotel.

That morning's outing was only the first of several Ben was asked to share in the week that followed – excursions to the royal palace at Caserta and the excavations at Pompeii, as well as an evening at the vast opera-house of San Carlo. Ben was at first in despair, realizing that after a day or two he could never afford his share of the expenses, but Mr Cooper took him aside in the discreetest possible manner, assuring him that it would be a personal favour to him if Ben would join them. The Neapolitan *lazzaroni* were a most truculent horde of cut-throats – Mrs Cooper was of a nervous disposition, and the presence of a powerfully-built young Englishman would make all the difference to her enjoyment of the sights. Mr Cooper also expressed a growing interest in art. Ben's sketches delighted him, as they did his wife. So, without any precise bargains being struck, an understanding was achieved: Mr Cooper provided the carriage and the wayside refreshment, while Ben from time to time presented a gratified Mrs Cooper with a sketch of some view she had particularly admired.

From this happy arrangement developed another project.

'Now,' Mrs Cooper announced, 'we can consider Paestum.' She fixed Ben with her eye. 'You know about Paestum.'

'I'm afraid not, ma'am.'

'There are the most wonderful ruined temples. They had been entirely overgrown by vegetation, lost for centuries. They were discovered when a new coach-road was being cut.'

'It is sixty miles, my love,' ventured Mr Cooper, 'and a somewhat remote region—'

'No matter! Mr Reeth will accompany us. Countless people have seen the ruins of Pompeii – I question whether anyone in the whole of Massachusetts has been to Paestum!' Mrs Cooper's eyes gleamed. Ben could picture her returning triumphantly to Salem, not only with the first account of the wonderful temples but with his own sketches as evidence.

It was quickly agreed. With Mrs Cooper one might as well agree quickly, for one would have to eventually.

Not for her the shifty sort of *vetturino* who had brought Ben to Naples. The hotel-proprietor produced a much-recommended courier, Domenico. A post-chaise was engaged. Two other tourists were planning a trip to Paestum, a scholarly Swiss professor, Dr Haussmann, and his elderly Polish friend, Count Casimir. It was agreed that they should hire another chaise and join the party.

It was now the first week in March, the sky a cloudless blue, the southern spring almost ready to merge into summer. They passed Vesuvius and Pompeii once more, and then all was fresh and unknown. A rugged line of mountains barred their way, but by late afternoon they were over it, and descending steeply to the Gulf of Salerno. Even Mr Cooper was now quite converted to the plan. The grandeur of the scenery made up for the prospect of traipsing round still more ruins.

Salerno, just over halfway, offered a convenient halt for the night. For the first time Ben was sleeping under the same roof as Miss Blackwood. They were together every hour of the day. They were no longer just half of a quartet, making a specific excursion and almost compelled to remain in a group. Count Casimir and Dr Haussmann were attentive to Mrs Cooper, who was charmed by what she called their 'continental manners'. What with the Count's ancient nobility and the professor's culture, she was fully occupied. Carriage-seats were politely exchanged for some stretches of the journey, and more than once, to save the horses on the steeper hills, Miss Blackwood insisted on walking. This enabled her to pick flowers, or as Mrs Cooper termed it, to 'botanize'. And it enabled Ben to have some uninterrupted conversations with her.

It was the same that evening in Salerno, when Mrs Cooper was too fatigued to do more than view the outside of the Norman cathedral. When Miss Blackwood expressed a desire to peep into the picturesque back-streets, and then to see the fishing-boats streaming past the harbour-mouth in the dusk, Ben could only offer his escort and Mrs Cooper insist on her accepting it. She did so without demur.

It was, of course, very different from those evening walks in London with Sal. Miss Blackwood's manner was cool, detached, sometimes with a hint of inward amusement. She talked of what she saw in front of her, the style and possible date of a building, or some human oddity among the passers-by, or the gay music throbbing from the lighted interior of a tavern.

They did not enter one of those places, as he probably would have done with Sal. Miss Blackwood was a lady. He would not have suggested it. He knew how to behave. They were back at the inn before even Mrs Cooper could raise an eyebrow.

It had all been very correct. Yet it had been an hour that Ben would not have missed for worlds. They had laughed a lot. Fanny – as he now thought of her, but dared not call her –

had a sense of humour as refreshing as the breeze from the darkening sea.

In the morning their road turned away, disappointingly, from the shores of the gulf. They had mountains, romantic enough, to their left, but on their right a spreading green flatness, grazed by horses and buffalo.

'A bad country for fever,' said Dr Haussmann in his rasping English, 'but that will be later. In the full heat of summer. Do not disturb yourself, dear lady.' Mrs Cooper did not.

Time seemed to matter less and less as they drove slowly southwards. Mr Cooper, from sheer business habit, would still pull out his watch at intervals, but he seemed scarcely to take in what hour the hands indicated. There were no cities such as Naples ahead of them, hardly towns even, and little traffic but the occasional peasant's donkey or a military patrol.

'This is Arcadia!' declaimed Mrs Cooper. 'Surely, Mr Reeth – as an artist – you must feel that more than any of us?'

'Indeed I do, ma'am.'

Ben was sitting beside Fanny in the chaise at the time, so close that he felt the vibration of her stifled laughter.

Towards the end of the day the road brought them back towards the sea again. Paestum, thought the professor, must once have been on the coast. In two thousand years the shore had silted up, pushing back the sea for a mile or more. The famous city built by the Greeks was now stranded, its surviving columns dotted in a tangle of undergrowth that would take years to clear.

'I can believe that,' said Mr Cooper, 'especially the way folk seem to work, hereabouts.'

There was only one possible inn, and that left much to be desired. It reeked of cooking smells – and worse. Fanny wrinkled up her attractive nose with disgust. Domenico was full of apologies. Few foreigners penetrated to Paestum, especially since the war. One could not expect the elegance and convenience of the Neapolitan hotels.

They were not, however, the only foreigners there, although there were no other ladies. There were three swarthy, youngish Frenchmen. To Ben's observant eye their tail-coats and top-hats sat oddly on them. They had the bearing of soldiers – he remembered Pierre Arnauld. They would have been more at ease in tunic and helmet. All three sported violet ribbons.

The other tourists were two loud-voiced fops from Oxford, Lord Ludbury and the Honourable Rupert Forbes. They surveyed the rest of the company disdainfully at table, and kept to themselves. Ben could read in their eyes their immediate assessment. The Frenchmen? Frogs, mounseers, Bonapartists. The Americans? Americans. And Ben himself? Ben might puzzle them a little but they could place him more exactly in the English social scale than any of the foreigners could.

Two nights must be spent at Paestum, whatever the conditions. Mrs Cooper wanted to inspect the ruins at leisure, before facing the fatigues of the journey back.

So, in the cool of the morning, Domenico led them slowly through the green thickets, from one half-buried line of limestone blocks to another, and Dr Haussmann talked of the Greeks and the Romans and the Saracens, and tried to make Mrs Cooper see the difference between the Doric style and the Ionic. He wagged his beard mournfully over this once-proud city, where now only the lizards scuttled over the crumbling walls and the local goats pattered across the temple-floors on their neat, clicking hoofs, pausing to nibble at the prickly acanthus bushes. And all the time the unseen cicadas played their whirring music in the coarse grass.

'And once,' the professor lamented, 'Virgil tells us this place was famous for its roses – and its violets.'

'Bonapartist even in those days,' Ben whispered, and was gratified to see that Fanny was stifling a giggle. 'I am pleased to see,' he dared to add, 'you have been wearing other colours of late.'

'Not to please *you*, Mr Reeth. Fashions wear out. And those young Frenchmen last night – I should not wish them to imagine we were of the same mind on everything.'

'I should hope not,' said Ben under his breath.

After dinner, when most of the world slept, he resolutely

set out to make some drawings. Mr Cooper was so generous. The least he could do was to offer a few black-and-white impressions of this romantic spot.

Before long, he was conscious of Fanny sitting in an adjacent patch of shade. Raising her eyes from her book, she called: 'Do not let me distract you. It was so stifling in my room. But if I seem to be alone—' She stopped. He knew what she meant. In the most solitary places a pretty girl seemed to produce bright-eyed Italians out of the air. And there were the three Frenchmen, still at the inn, not to mention the Oxford pair.

'You won't distract me,' he answered, not quite truthfully. He was drawing furiously, with bold black strokes. 'But I am moving on to the Temple of Neptune. You will have to follow.'

'I will follow – sir,' she said meekly.

He worked hard. At supper-time he was able to present Mrs Cooper with half-a-dozen sketches. She was loud in her delight. The rest of the company had little choice but to come crowding round. Lord Ludbury and the Honourable Rupert inspected the drawings with supercilious expressions and offered patronizing comments. Count Casimir muttered incomprehensibly in Polish; Dr Haussmann would have liked the detail of the Doric columns more clearly brought out. The French were warmest in their compliments, but Ben saw that they were more interested in a closer study of Fanny than of his pictures.

She herself was equally aware of that, and he was glad to see that she did not welcome it. As they rose from the meal she murmured, 'It is still so hot. And—' She wrinkled her nose.

'Would you like to take the air outside? There's a moon coming up. The temples—'

'Oh, yes! We should see them by moonlight!'

She fetched a scarf and they slipped away. The dusk was warm, as the limestone ruins gave back the heat burned into them throughout the afternoon. A huge silver dollar of a moon was balanced on the line of the mountains. The temple pillars glimmered milk-white and ghostly amid the dark foliage.

They picked their way carefully. There were broken treacherous steps. There were great drums of stone, sections of fallen columns, half-hidden, just where they had rolled after some earthquake centuries ago. It was an eerie place where it came natural to link hands, and seemed unnecessary to let go again.

'I would not have missed this,' he said.

'Nor would I!'

'You don't think,' he suggested mischievously, 'we should have asked the Coopers?'

'Oh, no. Mrs Cooper would expect mosquitoes. And you know that Mr Cooper gets weary of ruins.' She laughed softly. 'He prefers what he calls "a going concern".'

They moved on in silence. They came to a clearer spot. A long row of fluted columns gleamed dramatically in the moonlight.

'A perfect back-drop!' he said, and went on, 'sometimes I wonder if I should be better at theatre scenery. The bold effect, you know. Sketches are well enough – if you work fast—'

'As you did today.'

'But when it comes to the patient, intricate detail—'

'Are you a patient person – Mr Reeth?'

'No! Oh, sometimes. I don't know.'

'Is there scope for an artist – I mean, a real artist – in a theatre?'

'Perhaps. A livelihood, anyway. But I am not "a real artist".' And the truth began to tumble out, unpremeditated. He explained his humble role at Covent Garden and the precise extent of his experience in a painter's studio.

She said little. Only once did she burst out, 'But what does all this matter? What a man *is* – that is what signifies.'

They lost track of time. They continued to move slowly across the surface of the long-lost city. In effect they saw nothing more of it that night, though they paused instinctively to stare at some feature and murmur a comment. They were thinking and talking of other things. The moonlit ruins left no further images in their memory.

Suddenly she cried out: 'Good heavens! We must go back. What will they be thinking?'

They walked as fast as it was safe to do over that obstructed ground. Her long skirt rustled as she sped through the gloom beside him.

'I can see the lights of the inn,' he assured her.

'Yes. And listen! Singing!'

Men's voices, robust and resonant, came loudly through the night. It was not the kind of singing they had heard from the taverns of Salerno. The words were not slurred. They had the beat of men marching in step. Fanny checked her pace suddenly.

'That's the *Marseillaise*,' she said sharply.

'Our French friends! Who were so smitten with you—'

She ignored that. 'That song is banned. They must be drunk to sing it here.'

'They don't sound drunk to me.'

The chorus ended. A single voice shouted: '*Vive l'Empereur!*' Then the little group roared in unison: '*Vive l'Empereur!*'

'Something's happened,' she said.

There was a whip-crack, so sharp and unexpected that Ben took it for a pistol-shot. Then he heard the creak of carriage-wheels and the clatter of hoofs as horses gathered speed. Lights went bobbing away down the road. They were out of sight by the time Ben and Fanny reached the door of the inn.

Mrs Cooper met them at the foot of the stairs, a crumpled newspaper in her hand. 'I think everybody has gone mad!' she complained. 'There is news from Naples – Fanny, you must translate it for us. It seems that Napoleon has escaped from Elba!'

16 Destination unknown

Fanny moved to the lamp and stared at the black print. She read aloud, rapidly:

'*It is reported from Elba that the Emperor quitted the island secretly on the night of Sunday, 26th February—*'

'A week ago!' said Ben.

'*He sailed in his ship* L'Inconstant, *with several smaller craft, accompanied by his troops amounting to about a thousand men. He appears to have eluded the blockade of patrolling British cruisers.*' Fanny's voice thrilled with her old enthusiasm, which had been less evident of late. '*The British Commissioner was absent at the time, visiting his doctor in Florence.*'

'But where has he gone?' demanded Mrs Cooper. 'Napoleon?'

'It doesn't say. *The destination of the Emperor and his intentions are unknown.*'

'We can guess at his intentions,' said Mr Cooper grimly. 'Europe may look forward to another long war.'

'This has been planned carefully,' said Ben, 'and for a long time.' He remembered the eagle button he had picked up on the wharf two months ago. A thousand men . . . only a handful against the armies of the Allies – but a beginning. The Emperor would not have gambled without the certainty of a good deal more. He turned to Mr Cooper. 'Where do you think he will make for?'

The merchant pursed his lips. 'I wouldn't be mightily surprised if he were in Naples by now.'

'Naples!' cried Mrs Cooper incredulously.

'Murat betrayed him,' said Fanny.

'True, my dear – but Murat's wife is Napoleon's sister. And Murat has other temptations to change sides again. His throne is not too safe. Some of the Allies want to bring back the Bourbon king from Sicily. So if Murat thinks Napoleon has a good chance, he won't hesitate long.'

Dr Haussmann had joined them and caught the last

remark. 'That is what our French friends are hoping,' he said. 'They say to Count Casimir just now — as soon as they know where to go, they hurry to offer their swords to the Emperor. Perhaps in Naples.'

Ben caught his breath. If Murat lined up with Napoleon, his thousand veterans would be transformed instantly into a sizeable army, and he would have one of his most brilliant generals at his side again. They would hold the southern half of the peninsula – not a bad base to start from! – and most of northern Italy would be at their mercy too. And, to judge from the signs of Bonapartist sympathy he had noticed throughout his travels, the three former officers in this inn would not be alone in rallying to their old leader.

'This is serious,' he muttered.

'Lord Ludbury seemed to think so,' said Mr Cooper.

Ben looked round. 'Where are those two?'

'They left – hurriedly. There was a great fuss, getting horses at this time of night.'

'But what is going to happen?' Mrs Cooper looked agitated.

The Swiss professor soothed her. 'There is no danger, madam. I have spoken with our good Domenico. He advises we stay here tomorrow – until the situation clarifies itself. Here nothing will happen. But if we return too soon to Naples—'

'There might be fighting! Bombardment! Those impulsive young Englishmen—'

'They are not going to Naples, madam. They have gone south. They hope to reach safety in Sicily.'

'*Safety!* What ever do you mean? This is all most extra-ordinary.'

'Not really, ma'am,' said Ben. 'You have nothing to fear – you are Americans. Dr Haussmann and the Count – I imagine they have no cause for concern. But Lord Ludbury is British—'

'So are *you*,' said Fanny. There was an edge to her voice.

'Yes. And if the King of Naples declares for Bonaparte—' Ben tried to speak in the casual, unruffled tone expected of his nation— 'British tourists may find things . . . awkward.'

'But you are with *us*!' said Mrs Cooper grandly.

'That might not be a complete protection, ma'am. The last time British tourists were caught in this way, some of them were interned for ten years—'

'Ten *years*?' Fanny echoed in horror.

'A thought which may have occurred to Lord Ludbury.'

'They might have waited for you – given you a chance to share their carriage! Those dressed-up, supercilious—'

Mr Cooper gently interrupted her. 'Mr Reeth is much safer here. If Murat sides with Napoleon, I doubt if those young men will get across the straits to Sicily. Murat's dispatch riders will travel far faster than they can. And the first time they are asked for their passports—' He stopped, with a significant expression.

There was nothing to be done that night, except to cancel their departure for the next morning. The courier's advice made sense. A quiet spot like Paestum would not be involved in military operations. They should stay and await developments.

It was not comfortable advice for Ben. He retired to bed in a mental turmoil, and slept only fitfully. From Fanny's face at breakfast he could tell that she too had been restless.

There was no fresh news. The ruins slept in the morning sunshine as they had done for centuries. Apart from the goats and the lizards nothing stirred. Dr Haussmann prowled about as cheerfully as ever, far more interested in tracing the course of an ancient Greek street than in the development of the current situation. Ben, unable to listen to any more learned disquisitions, used his sketching as an excuse to disappear. Very soon Fanny tracked him down.

'What are you going to do?'

'I'm trying to think.'

After a silence she said vehemently, 'I *hate* to think of you in danger.'

He laughed dryly. 'So do I.'

'You make a joke of everything. You know – I don't want you to go away – but I have an unpleasant feeling that you should.'

'So have I. But before I do anything I'd like to know which way the cat is going to jump. If I may so describe your beloved Napoleon.'

'He is *not* "my beloved Napoleon"! He is a great man, of course – I admire his achievements. But it's you I am concerned for, just now. You might wait just too long.'

He nodded. 'I might. But I do not wish to run the wrong way. I wonder how Lord Ludbury and the Honourable Rupert are getting on.'

'You heard Mr Cooper's opinion. He gave little for their chances. But I suppose it was the best thing, to make a dash for Sicily. The British are there. Sicily will be safe – but it is a long way off . . .'

'Two or three hundred miles, Domenico tells me. On these roads! And still the sea to cross.'

'Yes,' she said dejectedly. 'You must not attempt it.'

'I haven't decided.'

'Please! It's unthinkable. Your papers betray you as English, you know little Italian, and – forgive me – I imagine you have not much money?'

'No need for imagination, there. Sad, sober truth.'

'We must think of something. We must.' He saw her hands clenched on her lap. 'You are *not* going to spend years as a French prisoner!'

'Perhaps we shall hear some more encouraging news today.'

But none reached them, encouraging or otherwise. The tension at dinner affected everybody. Appetites were poor. Afterwards, in the languid heat of the siesta period, the stillness seemed even more oppressive than it had been before.

Ben and Fanny found themselves together again – without any explicit arrangement – in a shady corner of the Temple of Ceres, talking in lowered voices. Suddenly they were startled by distant shots. She gasped with alarm, then apologized.

'How stupid of me! It is the Frenchmen. I saw them going towards the olive-grove – they said they were going to practise with their pistols.'

'I suppose it will relieve their feelings,' he said lightly. 'They find it even harder to bear the suspense.' But also, he thought, they have a motive for their target-practice.

'You know, these Frenchmen bother me . . .'

He pretended to misunderstand. 'So I've observed! You must not let them embarrass you. These Frenchmen can't see a pretty girl without trying to flirt with her.'

'I can deal with that,' she said impatiently. 'I mean, they *frighten* me. Especially the very dark one. Major Costar.'

'Why?'

'I think he has only just realized you are English. Being with us, you were taken for an American. Not knowing English, they cannot tell the difference. And they cannot imagine that an American girl would understand much of their French.'

'You've overheard something?'

'Only vague murmurs. But if we get news that the Emperor *has* arrived in Naples—'

'They'll rush to join him. They make no secret of that.'

'And they will take him a gift – an English prisoner.'

'I see,' he said thoughtfully.

'Promise me—'

'Yes?'

'Keep your bag packed. Have your papers with you, and all your money. At all times. Be ready to leave instantly.'

'I have been. Since last night.'

She stood up. 'I will leave you now to your sketching.'

'I never felt less like sketching—'

'No, don't come with me. I want to talk to Domenico. And the people in the inn.'

She walked away. The pistol-shots continued to ring out from the olive-grove, followed by laughter and cries of derision.

He did not see her again until the evening, just before supper. He was changing into a clean shirt. Dr Haussmann and Count Casimir, who shared the room with him, had already tidied themselves and gone down. There was a faint, almost furtive, tap on the door.

'*Avanti!*' he answered without thinking,

The door opened a few inches. 'May I come in?' she whispered.

'Please—' Ben stepped back confusedly, thrusting the last fold of linen into his waistband.

She slipped into the room and closed the door silently. 'Forgive me! There's no time to think of the proprieties.'

'What happened?'

'Nothing – yet. Only a rumour from Salerno. Napoleon is expected in Naples. Is probably there by now.'

'Damnation!' He knotted his cravat. Suddenly he realized that she was holding his coat for him. He slid into it automatically. Afterwards he remembered how she had patted and smoothed the cloth on his shoulders. 'I shall have to decide something.'

'Something has *been* decided. And I must beg you not to argue.'

'What do you mean?' He spun round to face her. He had never seen a young woman look so determined.

'You must take supper – as usual. Everything as usual. Not a word or a look to betray anything. But then, while they are all sitting over their wine, slip out for a breath of air. Walk down the road. A chaise will be waiting under the trees.'

'But—'

She laid her fingers softly on his mouth. 'I said: *do not argue*. It is all arranged. If you don't go now, it will be too late. Oh, I know all the problems. I've tried to provide for everything.' She drew a folded paper from her reticule. 'You will not get far as an Englishman. You will have to travel on *my* passport.'

He stared at her. If her manner had not been so intense he would have burst out laughing. He merely said: 'That will hardly deceive a policeman. Do I *look* like "Fanny Blackwood"?'

'Don't waste time,' she begged. She opened the document and pushed it impatiently under his nose. 'You see? I am set down as "*Frances Blackwood*". How many Italians will know the difference between "Frances" and "Francis"? Their own name, "Francesco", has the "e". They would need to know

English, and to read it very carefully, to see that this paper refers to a female.'

'But what will *you* do for a passport?'

'My problem is nothing compared with yours. I can answer all your questions – but not now. I will wait beside the carriage. Promise me you will do as I say.'

He hesitated. 'I *shall* see you again? I mean, apart from meeting at supper?

'Of course. I shall be there. At the bend in the road. I will explain everything – I have worked it all out. But if I stop here a moment longer it may ruin everything.' She went back to the door and listened carefully. 'Put everything in your bag before you come down. You will find it in the carriage when you get there.' She listened again, opened the door silently, and was gone.

He stood, rubbing his chin. Then, with a shrug, he gathered up his soiled shirt and a few outstanding items, and packed them into the top of his portmanteau. The girl was probably right. He looked at her passport again, grinned, and folded it away. It might indeed be his salvation. He did not like taking it, but its loss to her was a trivial thing compared with its value to him. What, after all, could the Neapolitan authorities to do her? A young lady, and from the United States, a friendly country with which neither Naples nor Napoleon had any quarrel ... A young lady was permitted to mislay things, even passports ... The Coopers could vouch for her identity, the American Consul in Naples would smooth over any inconvenience and would provide her with fresh papers ...

Yes, he must accept her offer. And all the other arrangements, whatever they were, that she had made on his behalf.

The vital thing was to get away from here, where his British nationality was known. Then, somehow, make his way to Sicily. To return northwards would be to run straight into the arms of the enemy. He pursed his lips, calculating how much money he had left. Thanks to Mr Cooper, his recent expenses had been slight. But there would be little chance of selling more pictures as he went! By all accounts the long foot of the peninsula was a backward, impoverished region, where he would meet no art-loving tourists. In fact his own presence there might surprise the police. He would just have to wave Fanny's passport at them and remember that he was 'Frank Blackwood' from Salem.

He took a deep breath and went down to face the others at supper.

He felt bad about it. He could only hope that afterwards, when the girl explained to them, they would understand. It would be fatal to tell Mrs Cooper that he was going. Her exclamations and objections and counter-proposals would re-sound throughout the inn. He would have liked a quiet word with her husband, but decided against it. It would be unfair to Mr Cooper. Mrs Cooper would be furious with him for know-ing the secret and not sharing it.

Ben tried to behave as though this was just one more meal together, and not the last. He could not help saying to Mr Cooper, however, and hoping that his words would be remem-bered later: 'I can't tell you, sir, how grateful I am to you for bringing me here. I would not have missed Paestum for any-thing. But then, you and Mrs Cooper have been so extremely kind all along – and generous—'

He caught Fanny's eye across the table. Her look warned him not to lay it on too thick.

'It's nothing, my boy,' said Mr Cooper. 'Forget it.'

But his wife said, preening herself: 'It is for the wealthy to provide patronage for the arts.'

She went on for some time. She was apt to. His eyes strayed, like his thoughts, to the three Frenchmen at the end of the table. They were drinking hard and gabbling away with a devilish kind of gaiety. Somehow the lamplight made them look sinister – it turned their sallow faces paler, etched their eye-sockets and cheekbones with still blacker shadows, gave a more diabolical twinkle to their watchful eyes and an extra arrogance to their bushy whiskers and moustaches.

Was it his nervous fancy, or were they eyeing him with particular intentness?

It was near the end of the meal. People were toying with

fruit and nuts. Fanny stood up suddenly, with a murmured apology to Mrs Cooper. She had a headache, and would go to bed early. Ben had a heartache as he watched her go. Mrs Cooper was now holding forth to Dr Haussmann. He could bear the thought that, after this evening, he was unlikely ever to see Mrs Cooper again. The same thought, in respect of Fanny, was less agreeable.

He gave her a few minutes start. Then, as casually as he could, he made his excuses and left the table. Mrs Cooper, in full flow, acknowledged his going with a curt inclination of the head. The Frenchmen had already quitted the room, so they were not there to note his movements.

Outside the inn, the road stretched white under the full moon. Still casual, as if seeking nothing but fresh air, he began to stroll towards the dark cluster of trees a few hundred yards away. The whiff of cigar-smoke should have put him on his guard, but his mind was too desperately filled with other thoughts. He was taken completely by surprise when two figures stepped from the shadows and barred his path. Major Costar and one of the other Frenchmen.

'Monsieur Reet'?'

'Well?'

The conversation which followed was brief, and even Ben's scanty French was sufficient.

'You are British, we understand, not American? Be good enough to show us your papers.'

'Certainly not. You have no authority here.'

'We shall see about that. We hold the Emperor's commission. And the Emperor has returned.'

'That is nothing to me.'

'I think you will find that it is,' said the major. 'You will hand over your passport, monsieur. We wish to make sure that you will not leave this place without our knowledge.'

'Very well. You have no authority, but – as you wish, Major. My passport is in my room. I will discuss the matter with you later. First, I take my walk. In half an hour, Major – at the inn—'

And, with a show of mingled dignity and indignation, Ben tried to walk on.

'I think not,' said the other officer unpleasantly, and grabbed his arm.

It was an unwise move. Ben disliked people who laid hands on him. And his own hands were usually bigger and stronger. The Frenchman was of only medium height. Ben lifted him clear of the ground, shook him vigorously, and threw him – not hard, but contemptuously – into a spiky bush which would break his fall but give him cause to remember it.

'Ah!' cried the major triumphantly. 'Consider yourself—'

Ben did not consider anything, except that this interruption had gone on long enough. He hit the major just as he had hit Sir Henry a few weeks before. Costar went sprawling into the ditch. Ben wheeled round in time to see his other adversary emerging from the bush. A pistol-barrel gleamed in the moonlight. Before even the hammer could click into position, Ben landed a punch and sent the Frenchman hurtling back into the undergrowth.

He could not cope with both of them – not if they had pistols – and at any moment the third one might appear. He bolted. He heard their breathless shouts behind him. A pistol cracked, then another. Too fond of popping off their pistols, these Frenchmen! And it was no target-practice, this time.

He raced towards the bend. Thank God! There, a dim shape under the overhanging branches, was the carriage with a driver ready on the box, his face a pale blur turned to look back.

There was no sign of the girl standing in the roadway. But, as he drew level, she called tensely through the open door: 'Jump in! Quick! Are you hit?'

'No,' he gasped.

'Thank God!' She made no move to get out. As he flung himself on to the seat beside her, she cried sharply: '*Avanti!*'

'*Si, signorina! Presto!*'

The carriage sprang forward.

17 A drive by moonlight

'That was Major Costar?' she asked as they went swaying and clattering through the mesh of moonlight and shadows.

'Yes. You were right,' he said gratefully. 'It was time for me to go.' As his breath came back, so did a wider realization of their position. 'But *you*—' Raising his voice, he told the driver to stop.

'*No, no, Guido!*' she shouted. '*Avanti!*'

'*Si, signorina!*'

The man drove on without slackening speed.

'But you must get back,' he protested. This had not been in the plan. Those wretched Frenchmen had upset everything.

'Do you want me to walk back along this road – alone – at this time of night?'

'Of course not!' They must have covered a mile by now. 'You must use the carriage. I can walk from here.'

'Don't be a fool,' she said sharply. 'I have taken a lot of trouble—'

'Thank you—'

'Thank me by not ruining the arrangements now. How far would you get on foot? Alone? Speaking very little Italian? I am sorry,' she went on, her tone softening. 'I sound like a governess.' She chuckled. 'But my nerves are on edge. I am not used to this sort of thing.'

'I should think not! I am quite appalled – involving you to this extent. As if it were not enough to have this carriage waiting for me – now, to get carried away yourself—'

Again she chuckled. 'Yes, I suppose I *have* been rather "carried away".'

'You're very light-hearted about it.'

'I'm a light-hearted person.'

'But you're in a serious predicament,' he said severely. 'We can't do anything here. But when daylight comes, and we find some safe respectable place, we must decide what to do. I must get you back to Paestum – the Coopers will be frantic—'

'You forget: I have retired to bed with a headache.'

'But in the morning—'

'They will find my note.'

He turned in his seat aghast. He could see only a dark profile, tilted defiantly. 'You left a note?'

'Of course! They have been so kind – although poor Martha has often driven me almost to distraction—'

'You *meant* to come!' he cried, accusingly. He bent forward and touched the dim shape he felt at his feet. This bag was not his. His own was on the seat opposite.

'You must be sensible.'

'*I* must be sensible!'

'There was not time to argue this out beforehand. And I had a feeling that you would not agree. You English can be so conventional. You would rather risk years in a prison-camp than endanger a young lady's reputation. So – I take full responsibility.'

'You may say that. All the same—'

'Please! Let me finish. I knew from the start – you know yourself, if only you would admit it – that your chances of getting away by yourself were very slight. Who can help you? If I don't?'

He had no answer.

'I suppose it is very forward of me. Unbecoming. But we are not in Massachusetts here, or England either. It seemed the only practicable thing to do.' She hesitated, and then added awkwardly: 'You mustn't misunderstand. You must believe . . . I am only being *practical*.'

'You have behaved wonderfully. I understand that. And I'm truly grateful. If rather taken aback.'

The horses were slackening pace. 'Why is he stopping?' she exclaimed anxiously. She called: '*Guido! Avanti!*' But the driver took no notice. He pulled up. Ben saw lanterns. They gleamed on helmets and buttons and epaulettes of gold lace. A suspicious voice was questioning Guido.

'They want to see your papers – Francis,' she whispered. He pulled out her passport. His own was stowed away where only a complete search would reveal it. 'It might look well,' she added, 'if we sat closer.' And she positively snuggled against his shoulder, which he would have enjoyed more if his mind had not been anxiously occupied elsewhere.

The lantern shone through the window. A gloved hand was thrust in, the passport taken, and after a brief examination returned. '*Americano*,' said the voice, now more interested than suspicious. '*E la signorina?*'

Ben's heart almost stopped beating. But from the face nuzzling his coat emerged a stream of impressively fluent Italian, at once reproachful and seductive. The officer laughed and muttered an apology. Amid a chorus of amiable good-nights the carriage drove on.

The girl sat up again. Ben said, admiringly: 'You got us out of that. I suppose I had better not guess what lies you told?'

'Well ... There is one thing all these Italians seem to understand. Love. I told him it was very ungallant of him to ask awkward questions at a moment like this. No Neapolitan officer would wish to be thought ungallant. You must be prepared to do it again.'

'I am more than prepared,' he said. The reaction had made him a little light-headed.

'I said there were not to be any misunderstandings—'

'Of course! Whatever you do or say is purely for practical reasons. Your acting – and your Italian – were superb.'

'Oh, my Italian is Tuscan – very different from what they speak here in the south. But at least it makes it harder for them to tell I am not Italian at all.' She laughed. 'If we'd been in Florence it would not have worked. There, I'd have had to pretend I was French, I suppose.'

'You'd have thought of something,' he said.

'I think you are beginning at last to have a little confidence in me,' she said teasingly. 'This young miss from Massachusetts.'

'You are—' He swallowed. 'Extraordinary.'

'Thank you, Mr Reeth. Mr Blackwood, I should say.'

They had left the coastal plain by now. The horses were plodding up a steep mountain road. He judged they must have covered about four miles.

'I have the utmost confidence in you,' he assured her

humbly, 'but I should like to know the next stage in your plan. You have realized, of course – the Frenchmen may come after us.'

'They will get no horses at this time of night,' she said.

'How can you be sure?'

'Domenico will see they don't. Domenico is devoted to me!'

'I can understand that. But how can he stop them?'

'He has explained to me. Here in the south all the people hang together. Throughout the ages the different governments have trodden them down – Normans, Aragonese, Bourbons, and lately the French. They have learned their own secret, stubborn ways of resistance. They recognize only one loyalty – to their own folk, above all their own relatives.'

'Then why should they help us?'

'For money. And I suppose—' She laughed. 'For love,' she continued. 'I mean, the love they imagine ... between us. They are not for the British, nor against Napoleon, but they are for romance. I do not wish to embarrass you, but you must help me to pretend. Domenico got it into his head that we were eloping—'

'*Eloping!*'

'I couldn't persuade him otherwise. Then I saw that it would be simpler to let him believe it. He would be so much more eager to help. It's the same with Guido. With luck, it will be the same with the rest of them. They will help us on our way. They will obstruct anyone trying to follow us.'

'It's a long road ahead,' said Ben.

'It need not be a road.'

'You mean, if someone with a boat ... ?' In his mind's eye he saw the riding-boot shape of Italy – they must be somewhere just north of the instep – and the great triangle of Sicily just clear of the toe. Palermo was on the north coast. In Palermo harbour, almost certainly, there would be British battleships.

'Domenico has told Guido to find us someone. It will be much safer than the road. Once at sea, we are untraceable. No innkeepers, no police patrols.'

It was logical. If he had been thinking only of himself, he would have agreed with more enthusiasm. But there was something so final – so drastic – about the scheme. She might well have added: once at sea there is no turning back.

'You think Guido is to be trusted?' he asked in a low voice.

'Domenico said so. Absolutely.'

'In *every* way?'

'In every way concerning us. Oh, I imagine these people have their own ideas about the law – they may be terrible rogues – but they have their own code of honour. If anyone is entrusted to their protection, man or woman, that person is safe.'

'I'm glad to hear it.'

He was still thinking to himself – however unwillingly – that if it were at all possible Fanny must return to Paestum. Heaven knew, he did not want to say goodbye to her, but if she would not think of her own future it was for him to do so. It was not only the Italians who had their code of honour. Miss Frances Blackwood of Salem was not for Benjamin Reeth of Somerset Alley, and she never could be. No one should say that he had acted like a penniless adventurer, pursuing a girl hopelessly above him, exploiting her impulsive nature until she landed herself in an impossible situation. No, she must go back to America without any scandal, and, as a first essential step, she must go back to the Coopers. By all means, let her help to put him on a boat that would take him across to Sicily. Then this trustworthy Guido must restore her to her friends.

Better, though, not to start an argument just now.

The carriage swung suddenly to the right, so that they lurched against each other. The wheels bumped and scraped over loose stones, then came to a halt. Guido dropped down from his box, opened the door, and reached for their bags.

'What's he saying?' Ben asked.

'The road is too bad now. We have to walk.'

It would have been hard to say whether it was a road at all or a dried watercourse. They stumbled after him. Through a rift in the cypresses the sea flashed at them, far below, the moon lifting a golden ladder to the horizon.

Guido struck off to the right again. A goat-path climbed and wound through the scrub. They could not go much further, Ben guessed, for they were now out on a kind of promontory. A jagged ruin, the shell of some ancient watch-tower, made a sudden blackness against the sky. Guido looked round to make sure that they were still following. Then he walked on through an archway. The bags thumped softly on flagstones as he set them down.

'*Signorina* . . .'

He conversed for some moments with Fanny. Their voices rustled oddly in that place. Ben stood, catching only a phrase now and then. 'Uncle Angelo' and 'tomorrow – without doubt'.

Then, before he realized it, the man was gone. They were alone in the musty gloom.

'Where in Heaven's name has he brought us?'

'It is called the Saracen Tower. It was built – long ago – to keep watch for Saracen raiders. He apologized. He could think of nowhere better. There is a village down there, but if we arrive there without warning, in the middle of the night . . .'

'I agree. Much safer here. But for how long?'

'He was not sure. He must find his uncle.'

'Uncle Angelo?'

'Ah, you heard. Uncle Angelo may be out with the fishing-boats. They come back at sunrise. Anyhow, he swears that once we are in the hands of Uncle Angelo, everything will go well.'

'I hope he's right,' said Ben. 'And I hope Uncle Angelo will have some food for us.'

18 Lone lateen sail

The invaluable Domenico had foreseen even this emergency.

Wedged between their bags was a small basket. Ben's exploring fingers closed round the neck of a bottle. A clean white napkin contained a loaf and cheese. There were apples and oranges, glasses and knives.

They sat outside on a stretch of broken wall, gazing over the sea. The air was soft and still. She had her long redingote and insisted that she was warm enough. It was too dark and eerie inside the tower, and it had too obviously been a favourite shelter for goats.

'We met at a picnic,' she said cheerfully.

'Yes. We were sitting on a live volcano then. There's a certain similarity, don't you think?'

'You're much too apprehensive. It's strange. I know how brave you really are.'

'If I'm apprehensive, it's for you.'

'You need not be.'

'Forgive me – but it's foolish to say that. You know what I mean. If people get a garbled account of this affair . . . it isn't likely they'll trouble to study all the complicated circumstances . . . I can imagine they gossip in Salem as they do elsewhere?'

She laughed. 'More! I wonder if ever I can live there again.'

'You see!'

'I am not thinking of scandal. I'm wondering if I wish to go back. I have breathed a wider air.' She spread her arms in a mock-dramatic gesture.

He was following his own thoughts. 'If only Guido would come back with some fresh news – that Napoleon was captured, or he'd gone elsewhere. Anywhere but Naples.'

'What would you do then?'

'Take you back to the Coopers. Make my apologies to them. And, if those Frenchmen are still about, tell them to go to the devil.'

'I think you would! And then, I suppose, I should never see Palermo. It is said to be so beautiful,' she said, half wistful, half mischievous. 'The mountains make a great curve around it. They call it the *Conca d'Oro*, the "golden shell".'

'You had better persuade the Coopers to take you there – respectably! Mr Cooper would enjoy the natural beauty.'

'How cross you sound! Lucky that we are alone. When we meet this Uncle Angelo, you must try to act more convincingly. Remember, this is a romantic elopement.'

'I'm sorry. I'm angry with myself. I've let you do all this on my behalf—'

'You could not help yourself.'

'Well,' he admitted, 'things have just happened.'

'Yes. Things have just happened.'

The moon sank, There was a dark, rather depressing hour, before dawn stole over the hills behind them and gave them their first clear idea of their surroundings.

The promontory offered a clear view of a rugged coast stretching southwards. Capes and coves went in and out alternately. They reminded Ben of the painted canvas flats he had so often set up at the sides of the stage. Below them lay a fishing-village: pink and terracotta cottages stuck to the cliff-face like so many birds' nests. A mole of heaped-up boulders was thrust out into the sea, making a small harbour. A line of fishing-boats with gracefully-curved, three-cornered lateen sails, was straggling in with the night's catch.

'I think we should not show ourselves,' Ben said.

They moved to the other side of the ruin. The sunrise splayed golden fingers across the sky. The village remained in a well of shadow, but soon the first direct beams were catching the cliff-top and the tower. The stonework gradually warmed.

'It's so peaceful here,' she said sleepily.

It was hard to believe in the world outside. Yet that world existed, Ben reminded himself grimly. At this very moment couriers must be galloping between the capitals of Europe, bugles were blowing in a score of camps, batteries of cannon were rumbling along the roads . . . Europe might already be at war again.

He wondered what everyone was doing. The Mulroys, he could well imagine, would be making post-haste for Calais, if indeed they were not already safely across the Channel. Jupp would be superintending the orderly evacuation of the establishment, counting every box and bag. Pierre Arnauld was probably back in uniform, the uniform of the emperor he had never in his heart abandoned. And Sir Henry? Sir Henry might be anywhere. Slashing himself a clear path of escape across the Continent, Ben could imagine; driving back all obstructive foreigners, whip in hand.

After an hour or two they saw a figure approaching the tower. They prepared to hide, but recognized Guido. He had brought them more food: dried fish, ham, a crisp warm loaf, another flask of wine. Ben caught the drift of what he said.

He had spoken to Uncle Angelo. The old man would take them. But they must wait until sunset. They must stay by the tower, and not show themselves on the skyline. Uncle Angelo would come for them. They had nothing to fear.

Guido himself was leaving them now. His horses were rested and he must return to Paestum, but he would not betray them.

'Is there news?' Ben demanded. 'Ask him – did he hear anything in the village?'

There was a brisk discussion, which Ben found hard to follow. Fanny explained.

'His uncle spoke with some sailors yesterday evening – a ship outward bound from Leghorn. There is panic in Rome. All the British have fled for fear of Napoleon.'

'Is he in Rome, then?'

'No one seems to know. It is all rumours. The most likely place is Naples, but the ship avoided Naples. His uncle thinks if the Emperor isn't there by now, he soon will be. So you did the right thing.'

'His uncle seems remarkably well informed – for an old fisherman in a place like this.'

She smiled. 'Perhaps he fishes for more than tunny.'

They paid Guido for his services and he departed with profuse good wishes for their future happiness.

The day passed drowsily. They were both feeling the loss of a night's sleep. The sun poured down on the stonework and the warmth came back at them comfortingly. They stretched themselves out on the dusty grass beneath the wall, pillowing their heads on their bags, talking and dozing alternately.

In mid-afternoon, prowling round the seaward side of the tower, he saw the ship. Fanny came running at his call.

'A frigate,' he said.

'How do you know?'

'The single band of white. One gun-deck. A ship of the line would have three.'

'Is it British?'

'Almost sure to be.' He clenched his fists in frustration. 'Two miles. It might as well be two hundred.'

The frigate continued on her course southwards. He watched helplessly until she was no more than a speck. He went back and flung himself on the ground again beside the girl. She was asleep again, breathing very softly, and slightly smiling, as though her dreams were pleasant.

Uncle Angelo presented himself at sunset. Ben had never met any one less angelic. He had a face of goat-like wickedness. Yet for all his tattered clothes and silver-bristled chin, he bore himself with dignity. A Prince of Darkness, thought Ben, if ever there was one.

'Can we trust him?' he murmured to Fanny.

'We have no choice.'

She conferred with the old man. He addressed her, Ben noted, as '*signora*', tactfully ignoring her lack of a wedding-ring. She turned back to Ben.

'He wants ten dollars now. The rest when we reach Palermo.'

Ben counted out the pieces of eight. Uncle Angelo pocketed them with the casualness of a duke picking up his winnings at cards.

Ben had insisted that on no account must they pay the

whole sum in advance, or even let the man know that between them they had the cash to do so. It would be an open invitation to betray them, perhaps even to cut their throats and drop them over the side. Fanny agreed. They must be wary.

Uncle Angelo seemed not to mind. Without more ado, he seized Fanny's bag and, with a courtly gesture, invited her to follow him. Ben went last, carrying his own portmanteau.

They took a path that zigzagged dizzily to the sea. Below them, the fishing fleet was already creeping out of the harbour. Like black fins the lateen sails unfurled, one by one, against the crimson backcloth of the west.

At the base of the cliff, bobbing at some weed-hung steps, was Uncle Angelo's felucca. About the size of a Gravesend barge, Ben reckoned, but faster-looking, less broad in the beam. A shadowy figure – a youth who turned out to be Uncle Angelo's grandson – stood up and handed them aboard. He took their bags and stowed them in the tiny cabin. In the gloom Ben could just make out a bunk each side, scarcely more than a shelf, with a pillow and a coarse blanket. His dismay increased as he completed a groping inspection of the vessel. It was poorly equipped for passengers.

'It's hardly fit for a lady,' he mumbled to Fanny.

'It isn't for ever,' she said. 'At least they have given up their own bunks to us. *And* their bedding,' she added with less enthusiasm. Then, her cheerfulness reasserting itself, she said: 'My redingote can hang as a curtain. I have been no more private in some of those Italian inns. And less so, driving through the night in a diligence.'

Carlo was casting off. When they came out of the cabin they found the sail spread darkly overhead. They were in open water.

Palermo ... The very name, thought Ben, was musical. There would be some practical problems there, but the danger of a French prison-camp would be over. There would be an American consul, who, if he could not arrange for Fanny to rejoin the Coopers, would put her on some suitable vessel bound for New England. Bankers and letters of credit ... a wonderful thing, money! It solved so many difficulties.

But however much Fanny had, he would manage somehow to settle his debt to her. Even a poor man had his pride.

Fanny was stifling a yawn. He himself was suddenly conscious that those cat-naps in the heat of the afternoon had not nearly made up for their sleepless night on the road.

'Well,' she announced. 'I am going to retire. Will you take the air a little longer?'

'Yes. Call me – when—'

'Of course.'

It was quite dark now, and the white stars beginning to twinkle. After a little while she called, and he went into the cabin, ducking to avoid a bumped head. The travelling-coat was hung along the side of her bunk and next to it her dangling dress brushed his hand as he stooped to take off his boots.

'Good night,' she said demurely from behind the improvised screen.

'Good night,' he answered reluctantly. He slipped out of his coat and wedged his long limbs into the opposite bunk, gingerly pulling the blanket over him. They did not speak again. But it took him longer than he had expected to fall asleep.

It was a shock to wake in the dawn and, peering out through the open cabin-door, to see a pearl-grey headland to port. He had hoped for an expanse of open sea.

'What's the matter?'

'Fanny!' He was startled to find her face, impish in the half-light, poking comically between the garments hung between them. 'I – beg your pardon—' he stammered.

'It is high time we used first names – or our friends out there will think us the most formal eloping couple in history! Why did you exclaim – before you saw me?'

'I can see land. We can't have reached Sicily.'

'No, that's still Calabria. The fishing-vessels prefer to hug the coast. Did you think he'd take us straight across?'

'I'd have felt happier.' He stared at the cliffs, stretching endlessly into the morning haze. 'All this is still Murat's country.'

'I think he knows what he's doing. But Ben, would you not care to study the Calabrian scenery more closely? I would like to ... tidy myself.'

He grabbed his boots and fled in confusion.

'*Buon giorno, signore!*' Carlo greeted him with flashing teeth. By the time Fanny emerged he had prepared a platter with sliced sausage and thick hunks of coarse brown bread. Uncle Angelo, it seemed, had no cooking facilities. No doubt his usual trips were short and coastal.

All that morning they held their course, giving a wide berth to each beetling promontory but seldom, even when crossing the intervening bays, sailing more than two or three miles off-shore. Uncle Angelo conversed volubly with his grandson, but Ben could not make out a word.

'It must be a dialect.' Fanny questioned the old man, and laughed at his reply. 'They're talking Greek,' she said.

'Why?'

'Remember, Paestum was once Greek. All this country was. And it seems that even after all these centuries some of their words linger with the fishermen. I asked him why. Do you know what he answered? "We speak Greek among ourselves, so the fish won't understand".'

'Or the foreigners?' Ben suggested. He could not share Fanny's faith in Uncle Angelo.

The felucca glided on. 'I suppose,' she said lazily, 'Aeneas and the Trojans came this way. Maybe Ulysses.'

'If Dr Haussmann were here, he'd tell us. At length!'

He would have appreciated this legend-laden scenery in less anxious circumstances. Just now, he would have been happier to see it fading astern.

In the late afternoon, to his dismay, Uncle Angelo changed course, swinging hard-a-port. Ben saw a buff and white town climbing the cliffs, with tall belfries and a castle above.

'He's taking us in!' he said.

Fanny called to the old man, standing like some sinister Charon at the stern. 'He says it's for fresh water,' she told Ben. 'And more food.'

'It wasn't in the bargain. I don't like it.'

'Nor do I. But what can we do?' Usually so cool, she was tense now. A cat sniffing danger.

Two stone piers, with iron beacons at the end, stretched out to meet them. The vessel crept between. Ben had an uneasy sensation of being swallowed by a monster.

Carlo made fast, hopped ashore, and went off with a wicker basket and an earthenware pitcher. Uncle Angelo scrambled on to the quay more stiffly, and vanished into some sort of warehouse.

'He said something about seeing a friend,' Fanny murmured.

'Some smuggling associate, I'd imagine. If ever I saw a rogue—'

'But a smuggler is the kind of man we need! Someone to run us across to Sicily without being challenged. So much better if he *is* a rogue – he's less likely to be hobnobbing with the police.'

'He might be, none the less,' said Ben cynically. 'Do them a favour by reporting the mysterious foreigners – and get favours in return to cover his smuggling activites.'

'I still trust him. But I shall be thankful when we get out of here.'

'There is just one thing . . .'

'Yes?'

'There might be later news here. I wish I understood more of the lingo. I'd take a chance, and walk along to those market stalls—'

'You must do no such thing!' Her hand was quick on his shoulder. 'Stay here. You mustn't be seen.'

'It's probably our last chance to hear what's happening—'

'All right!'

Before he could object, she had gone, pausing only on the edge of the quay to turn and signal fiercely that he should remain where he was.

His eye followed her proud, purposeful walk – she was easy to pick out, among the aproned, colourfully-costumed local women, going about their slow gossipy business on the waterfront. And he was not the only one watching her, he felt sure.

Her dress, her features made her as conspicuous as he would have been himself. A young foreign woman – an obvious lady – landing from a coasting craft ... she was *sure* to arouse curiosity. He could only hope that, as a girl, she would not be challenged. People were more likely to be suspicious of a man. She was safer than he would have been. But he wished fervently that she had not gone.

If she did not return in five minutes, he must go after her. She would be furious, but he was not going to sit tamely here while she ran into unknown troubles for his sake.

Here was Carlo, burdened with provisions and a brimming water-jar. He flashed Ben an amiable grin, stowed his purchases and composed himself for a doze.

Anxiously, Ben scanned the figures on the quay. Two policemen in Neapolitan uniforms came strolling past. They stopped, stared at the boat, and shouted to Carlo. The youth opened his eyes and called back an answer. The policemen seemed satisfied. They walked on, their scabbards jingling.

Thank God, here was Fanny! And the policemen had their backs to her, continuing their majestic progress along the harbourside.

Fanny was carrying an apple in each hand, bought at a stall no doubt to make a pretext for her visit. She was flushed with hurrying, her lips parted breathlessly. Linfoot would have painted her as Atalanta, racing with the golden apples ... Yes, that would have been a picture to stir the Academy!

She tossed Ben one of the apples, freeing a hand to steady herself as she stepped aboard again.

'Any news?' he asked anxiously.

He thought she hesitated. 'No – not really.' She bit into her own apple and, as she munched, it was hard to be quite sure whether there was indeed any change in her normal voice. 'I think we ought to leave as soon as Uncle comes back. I shall tell him – very firmly – there must be no more calls on the mainland. He must take us straight across.'

They sat on the edge of their bunks, eating the apples. He did not like to question her more closely. She was clearly uneasy. Had she heard bad news in the market, and would not tell him? He could only stare out at the sun-baked quay, hoping to see Uncle Angelo – and not the policemen – again.

Ten minutes passed. Here was the old man in his silver-buttoned jacket, his bright red sash and piratical headkerchief of the same colour, an unmistakable figure moving through the crowds with dignified, unhurried step. He was wiping his lips and had the air of one who had made a good bargain. He carried a small sack, which he deposited with great care in the hold.

Fanny broke into emphatic Italian. Uncle Angelo bowed and raised his hand. '*Si, si, signora! Presto.*'

Carlo cast off and manoeuvred them clear of the other craft. With an inexpressible sense of relief Ben saw the line of houses sliding astern. Now the two piers rose in front, the great iron baskets of their beacons harshly outlined, the open water glittering beyond. Impulsively he squeezed Fanny's hand. She answered the pressure. So he had been right: her relief was as great as his.

There was one nerve-racking minute before they cleared the harbour. The two policemen were lounging on the steps of the left-hand beacon, staring at the felucca as it approached. Ben pulled Fanny further back into the cabin.

Now the end of the pier loomed above them. One of the policemen shouted something. Uncle Angelo called back. The policeman waved a white-gloved hand in acknowledgment. As the vessel slipped by, Ben could have sworn that Uncle Angelo winked up at the uniformed figures.

Whatever his true relations with the authorites, there was nothing more, after that moment, that anyone ashore could have done to hinder them. They were clear of the harbour. Soon they would be no more than a dot on the south-western horizon, a lone lateen sail standing out into the Tyrrhenian Sea.

19 Finishing touches

'My! You're as prickly as this blanket,' said Fanny. Her tension was forgotten. She was laughing softly.

They had been some hours at sea, moving steadily, almost silently, through the darkness. That darkness somehow made it easier to talk as they lay wakeful in the hard bunks.

'I begin to understand better,' she went on. 'It's your pride. I *like* a man to be independent. In America we think a lot about independence.'

'I believe you once made a Declaration about it?'

'Now you're teasing *me*. And I won't have it. Not just now, anyway. When I'm trying to be serious, and set things straight, and remove misunderstandings. Whatever gave you this absurd notion I was wealthy – an heiress?'

'I don't know.' He spoke with some embarrassment, although he was conscious, for the second time that day, of a wonderfully liberating sensation that had flooded through him. 'I suppose it was your manner – and your friends—'

'Oh, Mr Cooper *is* very rich. That doesn't mean that *I* am.'

'You are rich enough to make this tour of Europe . . .'

'Not really. My father was a lawyer. He gave me a good education – he believed in it – but he left no fortune. You think I am practical, don't you?'

'Yes.'

'Sensible?'

'Yes! Well, usually.'

'My sister wouldn't agree with you. She seized on her half of the money – I don't blame her – but by now it must have melted away in mortgage payments and dull *sensible* things like that. She thought me crazy. To squander it all on one glorious madcap tour of wicked Europe! She quoted the Bible at me. I tell you,' said Fanny, 'by the time she'd done, I hardly knew whether I was a prodigal daughter – with no father to slink back to – or one of the unwise virgins. "You'll end your days teaching school," she told me. "No one will marry you," she said.'

'I think your sister exaggerated.'

'Oh, she did! She always does. I shan't be penniless when I get home. But maybe I shouldn't worry if I were. It was more important to make this trip. I don't regret it. I never will.' She considered for a few moments. 'But I do regret letting you get the wrong impression of me. You were so honest about yourself —the other evening at Paestum — I should have told you more about my own circumstances.'

'It was no business of mine.'

'Maybe not,' she said doubtfully, but something about the way she said it made him feel oddly elated.

Uncle Angelo was a good seaman. He knew how to make the most of the light winds and he could read the stars. In the morning Ben knew from the way the mast's shadow was slanting that the old man had kept his word. He was maintaining his course across the open sea to the north coast of Sicily.

The only land they caught sight of all that day was an occasional sun-bleached islet, its rocks almost dazzling in the glare. The Lipari Islands, explained Uncle Angelo. The black cloud in the distance came from the volcano, Stromboli.

'Our acquaintance *began* with a volcano,' said Fanny. She stopped abruptly. If she was unwilling to speak the obvious second half of her thought, Ben saw no reason to do it for her.

At sunset they could just discern the long black line of Sicily. Tomorrow morning, God willing, Uncle Angelo assured them, he would be setting them ashore in Palermo.

So for one more night they had to sleep as best they could in the stuffy cabin. When sleep deserted them, they talked in low voices. It was a good time to talk frankly and make up for earlier misunderstandings.

One point was not clarified until, safely landed in Palermo the next morning, Ben insisted that he take her at once to the American consulate.

The consul welcomed them cordially, heard their story with delighted interest, and said that they must tell it to his wife at dinner. 'A remarkable escapade!' he cried. Then he burst out laughing. 'But of course wholly unnecessary!'

'Unnecessary?' Ben echoed.

'You could not know, I suppose. Napoleon is not in Naples. He is in France. He landed at Antibes on the first of March. He proclaimed that he had come back to save France.' The consul picked up a paper from his desk. 'He says his eagles are once more upon the wing. *They will not rest until they perch on Notre Dame!*'

'The first of March,' said Ben dazedly. 'Then he was in France before we even knew he had escaped! And by the time we left Paestum—'

'He was marching on Paris. My latest information – you will understand the Bourbon censorship here is trying to keep it out of the newspapers – but my own information is that they haven't been able to stop him. France is rallying to him, the troops sent to arrest him have deserted to his side—'

Ben laughed and slapped his thigh. 'So all the time we were grilling under the sun and suffocating in that cabin, Boney was hundreds of miles away – and headed in the opposite direction!'

He turned round to see how Fanny was taking it, and caught a very odd expression on her face. She did not look surprised. She looked . . . guilty.

Realization dawned on him then, but it was not until some hours later, when they were alone again, that he was able to say accusingly, 'You knew that Napoleon was not heading for Naples! That he was actually in France. When did you find out? Was it when you bought those apples? And pretended there was no fresh news?'

'Yes,' she said, refusing to meet his eye. 'After all, it could have been another false rumour.'

'You knew it was true!'

She tossed her head defiantly. 'Maybe I did. Maybe I was just set on seeing Palermo. And didn't want you to take me back to Martha Cooper like a runaway schoolgirl.'

'Well, I'm damned,' he said.

'Shall we leave it at that?' Her tone discouraged further discussion of the matter, but there was laughter in her eyes.

For the next few days Ben saw the world around him through a shimmer of happiness and growing hope. There was no present chance of leaving Palermo. Ships' sailings were in confusion until the war situation became clearer. He lodged at a cheap inn while Fanny stayed as guest of the consul's wife, for propriety's sake.

They spent the days together, exploring the ancient Sicilian capital with its cool cloisters and palm-shaded gardens, and sometimes driving up one of the steep roads to enjoy the superb panorama of the mountain-girdled bay. Several times Ben nerved himself to speak of the future, but always as he drew in his breath before starting on such weighty matters, Fanny thwarted him with some light remark or suddenly exclaimed at the splendour of the golden mosaics or the Saracen pillars. It was almost as though she were willing him to speak of nothing but the present.

On the fourth day, however, when he made his usual morning appearance at the consul's house, she came flying into the room.

'Have you heard?' she demanded.

'What?'

'Murat has shown his colours! His armies are on the march. He has occupied Rome. Clearly he's supporting Napoleon.'

'Then there will be war again,' Ben said soberly.

'Maybe. But don't you see,' she said impatiently, 'we were right to make a dash for it? You would have been imprisoned if we hadn't. Now will you forgive me my one white lie?'

'On one condition.' It was now or never. Gently, but very firmly, he took her small hand in his own huge one. He tilted up her chin, making her look at him. No more evasion. 'That it is the last lie – in all our life together.' His tone was still sober, but he could not check the smile that twitched his lips. 'At least about things that matter.'

'Why, Mr Reeth,' she said demurely. 'Are you making me an offer? I must confess, sir – I do think it is *high time*!'

They reached London in May. Murat had already been routed by the Austrians at Tolentino. And a few weeks afterwards the city was ringing with the news that Wellington had smashed Napoleon's own army outside Brussels, at Waterloo.

Ben lost no time in presenting Fanny to Linfoot. The old artist welcomed them with open arms. And when they told him of the impending wedding, he puffed out his cheeks delightedly and suggested a glass of madeira by way of celebration.

'For, my dear Miss Blackwood, you are a beauty! I told this young rascal to go to Italy and study the antique. But he has the impudence to come back with *you*.' He surveyed her with appreciation. 'I must paint you,' he announced.

'I told you he would say that,' Ben murmured.

Fanny smiled. 'I am deeply honoured, Mr Linfoot. But we are to be married in three weeks – and then we have our passages arranged in a ship to Boston. I want Ben to try his fortune in America.'

'H'm. Pity! Never mind,' said Linfoot generously. 'This young fellow will fall on his feet somehow – he has done, so far! He'll have to struggle, but in the end he'll do well enough.' He turned and fixed Ben with a stern eye. 'Don't you go imitating Turner! No good telling you to study the antique. You'll go your own way, I know. But your drawing's come on famously since I last saw you.'

'Come on?' Ben echoed. 'How do you know, sir?'

'I've seen some of the sketches you did in France and Italy. Sir Henry showed me.'

'He got back to England all right, then?' Ben felt relieved.

'Bless my soul, yes. I've been painting his portait this past month. Like to see it? Come up to the studio. I'm just putting the finishing touches.'

They followed him upstairs. Sir Henry, as might have been expected, occupied the greater part of a large canvas. The background was a building which they both recognized.

'Elba!' cried Fanny. 'The Emperor's villa!'

'From the very angle that I sketched it,' said Ben.

'Of course!' said Linfoot. 'Sir Henry brought me your sketch as a guide. It tickled his fancy to be painted in this setting, gloating over Bonaparte in exile.'

'Impossible man!' said Fanny, 'and I *don't* mean the Emperor.'

Linfoot pointed to a tiny figure in the distance. 'That,' he chuckled, 'is your future husband. Sir Henry said, "Put young Benjie in for old time's sake – but cut him down to size".'

'The old devil!' said Fanny explosively.

Linfoot was mixing some paints. 'You shall have your revenge, my dear.'

He walked back to the easel, squinted at the tiny figure in the background, and began, with the swift confident mastery of a lifetime, to create an even tinier figure beside it. It was the work of a few minutes, a dab of white, a dab of pink, some longer and more fluid strokes of purplish blue, but the effect was magical. There, captured for ever on the canvas, was a girl in a violet dress.

'I said I must paint you, my dear. This must serve, until Ben brings you back to England.' The old artist chuckled again. 'I'll enjoy Sir Henry's face when he sees this. But he'll not dare to take his horsewhip to *me*.'